THE LAWRENCE FILE
AN AUNT BESSIE COLD CASE MYSTERY
BOOK TWELVE

DIANA XARISSA

Copyright © 2024 by DX Dunn, LLC

Cover Copyright © 2024 Tell-Tale Book Covers

ISBN: 9798873731183

All rights reserved.

No part of this publication may be reproduced, distributed, or transmitted in any form or by any means, including photocopying, recording, or other electronic or mechanical methods, without the prior written permission of the publisher, except as permitted by U.S. copyright law. For permission requests, contact diana@dianaxarissa.com

The story, all names, characters, and incidents portrayed in this production are fictitious. No identification with actual persons (living or deceased), places, buildings, and products is intended or should be inferred.

First edition 2024

❦ Created with Vellum

CHAPTER 1

"Bessie?"

Bessie stopped and looked around. The beach was quiet on the cool and windy September morning, but it still took her a moment to spot the person calling her name. When she recognised Pat waving at her from the doorway at the back of one of the holiday cottages, she waved. He beckoned for her to come closer.

"Good morning," he said as she approached.

"Good morning," she replied with a bright smile. "I feel as if I haven't seen you in ages."

The young man flushed. "I went across for my sister's wedding and then ended up staying for a bit longer than I'd planned. Maggie and Thomas said it was okay, though."

Bessie nodded. Maggie and Thomas Shimmin owned the row of holiday cottages that ran along Laxey Beach. The first cottage wasn't far from Bessie's cottage, Treoghe Bwaane, which had been her home for a great many years.

When Bessie had first met Pat, he'd been homeless and had been breaking into one of the cottages at night to shelter from the island's cold and rain. Bessie had introduced him to Thomas and Maggie, and they'd given him a job and a place to stay. He'd spent several months during the off-season painting the cottages to get them ready for spring. Once tourist season had begun, he'd continued to stay in one of the cottages, providing on-site management for the business. Bessie knew that Maggie hadn't been pleased when Pat had gone across for the wedding, worrying that he might not come back, but everyone was happy that Pat was having a chance to reconnect with the sister he barely knew.

"Did you have a good time across, then?" Bessie asked.

Pat nodded. "It was awkward at first, but after a while my sister and I really connected. We had a lot of the same experiences in foster care, and we did our best to remember our lives before we lost Mum. I never thought I wanted family. I mean, I can look after myself, so I told myself I didn't need anyone else, but now that I have Peggy in my life, I can't imagine not having her around."

Bessie smiled. "I'm so happy for you, and for Peggy."

He nodded and then looked behind him into the cottage. "She's here – staying here, I mean."

"Really?" Bessie was surprised.

Pat grinned. "When I told Maggie that Peggy and her new husband couldn't really afford a honeymoon, she suggested that they come and stay in one of the cottages for a few days. It took them some time to arrange to get off work together, but they finally managed it."

"How lovely for them."

"They'll only be here for a few days."

"What are you going to do when they go home?"

Pat frowned. "I'm going to miss Peggy a lot, but I'm going to stay here. Maggie and Thomas have done a lot for me. I have a good job and a place to stay. Maggie has taught me how to drive, and I'm going to start taking classes again next week. It would be foolish to give all of that up, especially since Peggy and I can talk on the phone and text whenever we want."

"I think that's very sensible."

Pat chuckled. "I've not been called sensible very often in my life."

"Pat?"

Bessie smiled at the young woman who'd walked into the room behind Pat. She didn't look much older than eighteen, and she was wearing fuzzy pyjamas, covered in a kitten print, and large white furry slippers.

Pat's smile lit up his face. "Bessie, this is my sister, Peggy."

The girl flushed and then looked down at her pyjamas. "I didn't realise we had company," she said. "I'm sorry. I can go and change."

"You don't need to apologise to me," Bessie told her. "I'm just very happy to meet you."

Peggy nodded. "Pat has told me so much about you. Thank you for helping him so very much."

"I didn't do all that much. He's done all the hard work himself."

Peggy smiled proudly. "He's a good person. He just needed someone else to recognise that and give him a chance."

"He's proven himself many times over," Bessie told her.

"I'm going to go and change. I'll be right back," Peggy said.

Pat and Bessie watched her leave the room

"That was my sister," Pat said with a small laugh. "I suppose you got that."

"I did. There's a very strong family resemblance."

He nodded. "She looks so much like our mother. She's beautiful."

"She is, indeed."

Pat shook his head. "But what is this I hear about a cold

case unit? I didn't see the article in the local paper before I went away, but it was all that Maggie wanted to talk about when we spoke while I was across."

"I can't really talk about it," Bessie said. "Everything that is public knowledge was in the article in the *Isle of Man Times*."

"I told Peggy all about it. She was very impressed that I actually know some of the people involved."

"I believe you know all of them, especially since some of them have stayed in the cottages here."

"Now that you say that, you're right. I was just thinking about the people I know who live on the island, but I've met everyone in the unit, haven't I?"

"I'm sure you have."

"But the other two police inspectors, they aren't staying in the holiday cottages this month."

Bessie shook her head. "They've gone back to the Seaview. While they appreciated having entire cottages to themselves, they've both decided that they'd rather have the housekeeping services and room service that the Seaview provides."

"I'd probably feel the same way if that was an option," Pat said with a laugh.

"Feel the same way about what?" Peggy asked as she walked back into the room. She was wearing jeans and a sweatshirt, and she'd pulled her hair back into a loose ponytail.

"We were just talking about the police inspectors who are in the cold case unit with Bessie," Pat explained. "They stayed in holiday cottages here for a few months, but now they've gone back to staying at the Seaview instead."

Peggy looked at Bessie. "Pat showed me the article about the cold case unit. I was surprised when he told me that he knows a few of the people in the unit, but here you are."

Bessie grinned. "Here I am."

THE LAWRENCE FILE

"What's it like? The cold case unit, I mean. After all my years in foster care, I tend to try to avoid the police, but you're working with them all the time," Peggy said.

"It's very interesting work, but everything that we do is confidential, which means I can't really talk about it," Bessie replied.

"But you've solved at least a few of the cold cases, right? That must be very satisfying," Pat said.

Bessie nodded. "We've solved some cases." *Every single one of them,* she added to herself. "And it is very satisfying, especially with murder investigations."

"I'm trying to remember what I read," Peggy said. "Pat said that he's talked to the man who started the unit a bunch of times."

"That's because Inspector Cheatham stays in the cottage on the end of the row every time he comes over. He's been staying there longer than I've been working for Thomas and Maggie," Pat explained. "He likes to stay in the cottage nearest to Bessie's."

Peggy nodded. "Pat pointed out which cottage was yours. It doesn't look anything like the others, of course. They're all very much the same. Pat said you've lived there for a long time."

"All of my adult life. I bought the cottage when I was eighteen."

"Wow. I can't imagine owning my own home. My husband and I don't think we'll ever be able to buy a house."

"Houses on the island were considerably less dear in those days," Bessie told her. "And I inherited some money when the man I was planning to marry passed away."

"Oh, that's really sad," Peggy said. "But if you've lived there ever since, does that mean you never got married?"

"I never did. I've always been quite happy on my own."

Peggy grinned. "I felt that way, especially after my

unhappy childhood, right up until I met Paul. I just knew, the first time we talked, that we were meant to be together."

"He's a good guy," Pat said.

"Good for you," Bessie said.

"But we were talking about Inspector Cheatham," Peggy remembered. "Pat said that he used to work for Scotland Yard."

Bessie nodded. "Andrew was a homicide inspector."

"And now he's investigating cold cases with you and a few others," Peggy said. "How did that come about? I'm not trying to be rude or anything, but you aren't exactly the sort of person I'd expect to find working on a cold case unit."

"It's a very unusual unit," Bessie agreed. "Although everyone else involved has at least some connection to the police. I suppose I was asked to join because I'd been involved in a great many murder investigations over the last few years. Andrew and I met during a murder investigation."

"Here on the island?" Pat asked.

"No, across. We were at Lakeview Holiday Park when a man was murdered."

"How dreadful. Did you find the body? Is that why you were involved?" Peggy asked.

"No, but the dead man was my friend's husband," Bessie said, trying to work out how best to explain the complicated situation.

Pat frowned. "How terrible for her."

"They were separated, and Doona had filed for divorce," Bessie explained. "But he'd arranged for us to visit the park, hoping for a reconciliation."

"I remember reading something about that in the article about the cold case unit," Peggy said. "Didn't your friend, Doona Moore, inherit the park, or something like that?"

"She inherited half of the park. She spends a lot of her time helping to manage the park from afar."

THE LAWRENCE FILE

"But she's part of the cold case unit, too, isn't she?" Pat asked.

"She is."

"Did she work for the police before she inherited a holiday park, then?" Peggy wondered.

"She was a receptionist at the station in Laxey," Bessie told her. "We met when she first moved to Laxey from the south of the island. Her second marriage had just broken down and she wanted a change of scenery."

"I don't want to be rude, but how old is she?" Peggy asked.

"She's somewhere in her forties," Bessie replied. "I don't think age is something that anyone should worry about, though."

Peggy nodded. "I couldn't wait to turn eighteen so that I could get out of the care system, but now that I'm out, I don't really care how old I am."

Bessie had stopped worrying about her age once she'd received her free bus pass. She reckoned that she was somewhere in the later part of middle age, and she was determined not to give the matter any additional thought until she received a birthday card from the Queen.

"Doona is very nice," Pat said. "I bump into her all over Laxey. A lot of the time she has one of John Rockwell's kids with her. Sometimes she has both of them."

Bessie nodded. "She does as much as she can to help him with Thomas and Amy."

"I'm lost," Peggy laughed.

"Inspector John Rockwell is another member of the cold case unit," Pat told her. "He's in charge of the police station here in Laxey, but he's from across somewhere. I don't know how long he's been on the island."

"He's been here over three years," Bessie said. "I met him right after he moved across, and we've been friends ever since."

"And he has two children?" Peggy asked.

"Yes, Thomas and Amy. Thomas is off to university any day now. He's decided to go to a school in Manchester. That's where the family lived before John took the job on the island," Bessie told her.

Peggy frowned. "Pat said that Doona helps with the children. Is their mother in Manchester?"

Pat shook his head. "I told you about her," he said. "She and Inspector Rockwell got divorced, and then she married the doctor who'd been treating her mother. They went to Africa for their honeymoon, and she died under mysterious circumstances."

Peggy looked at Bessie. "Really? Is all of that true?"

"Unfortunately, it is true," Bessie confirmed.

"I didn't think people died under mysterious circumstances in real life," Peggy said. "No one I know has ever died under mysterious circumstances."

"Thankfully, it doesn't happen very often," Bessie said.

"So Inspector Rockwell is part of the cold case unit, and he's in charge of the Laxey station, and he's raising two kids on his own?" Peggy asked.

"Yes to all of that, but Doona helps when she can," Bessie replied.

Peggy frowned. "How old is Inspector Rockwell? Are he and Doona a couple or is she just being nice?"

"John is also in his forties. He and Doona have been seeing each other for a while now," Bessie said. "Only they know how serious their relationship is, though."

"Wasn't there a much younger policeman in the unit, too?" Peggy asked.

Pat grinned. "Hugh Watterson. He's just a constable, but he's smart and he's also really nice."

"Didn't you tell me something about his wife?" Peggy asked her brother.

"Yeah, his wife, Grace, does some tutoring at the college. She's only there a few hours each week, because she has a little one, but she was the person who finally got me to understand a little bit of algebra."

"Grace was a primary school teacher before she had Aalish," Bessie added. "I didn't realise she was tutoring at the college, though."

Pat shrugged. "Like I said, she's only there a few hours a week. She said something about how her mother loves having the baby all to herself, so she decided to let her mother have some time with the baby and to do something useful with that time."

Bessie nodded, wondering if Grace would keep tutoring after baby number two arrived in February, but not voicing her thoughts.

"I'm trying to remember what I read," Peggy said. "Is that all the unit members from the island?"

"It is," Bessie said. "The other two members come across from London for our meetings. Andrew does, too, of course."

"So who are the other two?" Peggy asked.

"Inspector Harry Blake and Inspector Charles Morris," Bessie told her. "They're both retired from Scotland Yard. Harry was a homicide inspector. Charles was an expert in missing persons."

Pat nodded. "I only talked to Harry once or twice, aside from giving him his keys each time he came over. He wasn't ever rude, but he was always abrupt and never wanted to chat. When his telly broke, he called and told me that it wasn't working, but then said that he didn't want me to come over and repair it until after he'd gone."

Peggy frowned. "Imagine living without a working telly."

Bessie grinned. "I don't have a telly."

Peggy's jaw dropped. "What do you do with your time?"

"I've never had trouble filling my time. I love to read, and

I've spent years working as an amateur historian as well. I read and transcribe old documents for the Manx Museum Library. I have friends with whom I enjoy spending time. I like to visit the island's historical sites, and I enjoy shopping trips and going out for meals."

"I wish I liked to read," Peggy said with a sigh. "I'm afraid I find it a chore."

"You need to work out what sorts of books you want to read," Bessie told her. "Once you do that, you'll find you love reading."

"She's right," Pat said. "She's made me love reading, and I used to hate it."

"I'd be more than happy to lend you a few books," Bessie said. "Maybe, while you're here, you can start to work out what genres you enjoy."

Pat laughed. "She is on her honeymoon," he said. "Maybe this isn't the best time."

Bessie felt her cheeks redden. "The offer is good whenever you're on the island," she said.

"When the other inspector stayed here, was he friendlier?" Peggy asked Pat.

He shrugged. "A bit, yeah, but there's something sad about him. Inspector Blake has world-weary eyes. Inspector Morris has sad eyes."

"You're very observant," Bessie said, agreeing with Pat's assessment of the two men.

"You learn to be in foster care," Pat said. "I moved around a lot. You learn how to read people for your own protection."

Peggy nodded. "I didn't get moved around as much as Pat, but that's because I learned to keep my mouth shut and keep my head down. Pat was too stubborn for his own good."

Pat shrugged. "I was angry at the world, and I took it out on everyone. I was fortunate that a few people believed in me, regardless."

"And now you know police inspectors and business owners, and you're in school, learning things so you can have a better future," Peggy said proudly.

Pat flushed. "And it's all thanks to Aunt Bessie."

Bessie shook her head. "You've worked really hard to get where you are today, and I know you're going to keep working hard and that you're going to accomplish amazing things."

"That's my brother," Peggy said happily.

"I hope you enjoy your stay on the island," Bessie told her.

"I'm sure we will. I know Pat would love for us to move here, but my husband and I both have good jobs back home. We'll just have to visit a lot."

"Maggie and Thomas have said that they're welcome to come and stay any time the cottages aren't fully booked," Pat said. "Which means they can visit pretty much any time of the year, aside from the busiest summer months."

"That was kind of Maggie and Thomas," Bessie said.

"They've been great," Pat said.

"They took us all out for dinner the first night we were here," Peggy said. "I had never eaten at such a fancy restaurant before."

"It was really nice," Pat said.

A buzzing noise made Bessie jump. Pat pulled out his mobile phone.

"Speak of the devil," he said with a grin. "Hello?"

Bessie smiled at Peggy as Pat walked away with the phone pressed to his ear.

"How long are you going to be staying on the island?" she asked the girl.

"Just two more nights. I wish we could stay longer, but Paul and I both need to get back to work. We're already planning for a big family Christmas here, though. I'm trying to find our older sister. Pat and I would both love to see her again."

"That would be nice."

"I'm not sure she wants to be found," Peggy said softly. "She told me years ago that once she got out of the system, she was going to disappear and start a whole new life where no one knew her or knew anything about her past. I don't blame her for feeling that way, but I miss her."

"If you need any help finding her, I may know someone who can help."

Peggy grinned. "I'm not sure we should have a bunch of Scotland Yard inspectors looking for her, but I may ask for your help anyway. I have a few friends to talk to first, though, people who were in the system with her. I think we'll be able to track her down."

"Good luck."

"That was Maggie," Pat said as he walked back across the room. He stuck his phone into his pocket and then shrugged. "Thomas isn't feeling well this morning, so Maggie isn't going to be able to come down and help with today's departures and arrivals. She suggested that you might be willing to help," he told Peggy.

She looked surprised. "Help with your work?"

Pat nodded. "She said she'll pay you for your time, and that you don't have to if you don't want to, but if we get several guests departing and others arriving at the same time, I might need some help."

"Is that likely?" Peggy asked.

Pat laughed. "We have two guests leaving and three guests arriving today. The departures are all supposed to happen before eleven, and the new arrivals can arrive at any time after midday and before midnight. It seems unlikely that anyone will overlap, but I suppose it's possible."

Peggy glanced at the watch. "It's only half seven. I can

probably be presentable in an hour or so if you want me to help."

"You can sit in the office with me this afternoon, anyway," Pat suggested. "I'll get the cleaning done in the two cottages with departures and then we just have to wait for the new arrivals. You and Paul didn't have plans for today, did you?"

"My plans for the visit are just to spend as much time with you as possible."

Pat nodded. "Next time they come over, we'll have you suggest some sights they should see," he told Bessie.

"I'd be happy to do that," Bessie told him. "But for now, I should get back to my walk."

Peggy gave her a quick hug before Pat gave her a longer one.

"It was nice meeting you," Peggy said.

"Likewise. I hope you enjoy your stay," Bessie replied.

She walked back down the sand towards the water and then stopped to look back and wave at the brother and sister, who were standing at the back of the cottage, watching her. They both waved before they shut the sliding door and disappeared from view.

CHAPTER 2

Bessie walked as far as the stairs to Thie yn Traie, a huge mansion that was perched high on the cliffs above the beach, and then turned and began to walk back towards home.

As she got closer to the holiday cottages, she glanced at the very last one in the row. As far as she knew, that was still where Pat was staying. Maggie and Thomas had stopped renting that cottage out after a second murder had taken place there, but Pat hadn't minded the cottage's rather gruesome history. He'd been grateful to have a place to stay. Perhaps, now that the busy summer season was over, he'd move into one of the other cottages, though.

Still thinking about Pat and his sister, Bessie walked the rest of the way back to Treoghe Bwaane. As she passed the cottage closest to hers, she noticed a family of five just exiting the cottage.

"We have to be out by eleven, anyway," the woman was saying.

"It's not even eight. We could leave our things here, go

and get breakfast, and then come back and pack," the man with her replied.

"Except with these three, we'd never get back in time," the woman snapped, nodding towards the children, who looked to range from the ages of three to ten.

"I don't want to go home," the middle child said in a whingy voice.

The smallest child immediately burst into tears. The oldest rolled his eyes and then turned and headed towards the water, walking briskly.

"Maelstrom, you get back here," the woman shouted.

Maelstrom? I must have misheard her, Bessie thought as she picked up her pace, eager to get to her cottage before anyone noticed her.

"I want to play, too," the middle child said, racing after her brother.

The baby just cried even louder.

"Maelstrom, Hiawatha, get back here this instant," the woman screamed. She looked at the man. "Put the bags in the car and then get Bob into his car seat. I'll get the other two."

Bessie unlocked her door and went into her cottage. "Maelstrom, Hiawatha, and Bob?" she said under her breath. "How unusual."

She poured herself a bowl of cereal and then added milk and some fruit. While she was waiting for the kettle to boil, she ate her cereal. After drinking her cup of tea, she slowly opened her front door and peeked outside. The little family was gone, and Pat was at the door to the cottage next to hers.

"Going to get it ready for your friend," he called to Bessie. "He'll be here this afternoon, right?"

Bessie nodded. "Some time after three," she called back.

He grinned. "I'll have everything ready for him in plenty of time."

Bessie shut her door and then looked around her small

kitchen. She washed her breakfast dishes and then tidied the room before heading into the sitting room. There she curled up with a good book and read until it was time for lunch. After lunch, she finished the book and then decided to take another walk while she waited for Andrew's arrival. He found her strolling along the sand a short while later.

"Hello, hello," the handsome, grey-haired man called as he walked down the beach towards her.

"Hello," she said. "I hope you didn't try knocking on my door."

He shook his head. "I spotted you as I drove up. It's a beautiful day for a walk on the beach."

"September is usually very wet, but today is lovely."

When he reached her, Andrew pulled Bessie into a hug. "How are you?" he asked as he released her.

"I'm fine. How are you?"

"I'm fine."

Bessie frowned. Andrew had been having some health issues lately and she knew that he was due to have surgery at some point in the near future. The last she'd heard, his doctor was allowing him to travel to the island for the cold case unit meetings only as long as he brought a travelling companion with him so that he was never alone. "But how are you, really?" she asked.

Andrew sighed. "I'm doing okay, really. My doctor is happy that things are stable, which is the best I'm going to get for now. It looks as if the surgery he wants to perform is going to wait until next year now."

"And is that good news?"

Andrew laughed. "I think so. I suspect Helen might prefer that I get it out of the way sooner, but she's been kind enough to agree to travel back and forth with me for the rest of the year. It helps that she's come to love the island, of course."

THE LAWRENCE FILE

"What about her job?"

"They've agreed to her working from here for a fortnight each month for the rest of the year. She'll probably spend most of every day on her mobile, dealing with everything, which means less time for sightseeing, but she's happy with the arrangements."

"That's good to hear."

"She said she'd rather work from here, staring at the sea, than sit in her cubicle back in London, staring at the row of cubicles around her."

"I can't imagine." The stipend that the cold case unit paid Bessie made it her first-ever paid job. After she'd bought her little cottage, her advocate had invested what was left of her inheritance. Bessie had spent years being incredibly frugal in order to make that small amount last for as long as possible. Her advocate had done a good job on her behalf, and she now had a considerable amount in the bank, but she still rarely indulged in anything more extravagant than an occasional hardcover book.

As the pair walked along the beach, they caught each other up on everything that had happened in their lives since Andrew had last been on the island. As they reached Treoghe Bwaane, Bessie had questions for her friend.

"The last time you were here, you said you had a really difficult case for us this month," she said. "Are we actually tackling that case, or did you find a different one for us to consider?"

Andrew made a face. "I decided that we should look at that case, but I'm really second-guessing myself now that I'm here. It appears almost impossible."

"All of our cases have been difficult."

"Yes, but this one is difficult on a different level."

"Oh?"

Andrew frowned. "You know I can't tell you anything

about the case until the meeting tomorrow. That isn't fair to the rest of the unit."

Bessie thought about arguing but decided not to bother. If the case truly was going to be that difficult, she didn't mind waiting, anyway.

"So let's talk about what really matters. What about dinner?" she asked.

"Let's go somewhere different," Andrew suggested. "Maybe we can find somewhere Helen hasn't been yet."

"What about somewhere in Peel?" Bessie said. "I have a friend whose daughter just opened a restaurant there a few months ago. I've been promising to go and have dinner there, but I haven't managed it yet."

"So it will be somewhere new for all of us."

"Exactly."

A few hours later, Bessie and Helen were passengers in Andrew's hire car as he drove them across the island towards Peel. Bessie was becoming increasingly fond of Andrew's daughter, who was kind and intelligent and took good care of her father. The restaurant was near the House of Manannan museum and had wonderful views of Peel Castle. The trio enjoyed the food, the atmosphere, and the conversation over dinner.

"That was lovely," Helen said as Andrew pointed the car towards Laxey.

"It was better than I was expecting," Bessie told her. "I knew the owner when she was a child, and she was a very fussy eater."

Helen laughed. "Maybe she doesn't eat all of the things on the menu."

"Maybe not. If she'd written the menu when she was six, there would have been a lot less on it."

"My oldest hated everything green when he was small," Helen told her. "But he did eventually outgrow it."

As Andrew drove them back to the parking area outside of Treoghe Bwaane, the trio talked about Helen's children. Once outside of Bessie's cottage, Andrew parked the car and they all got out.

"I have a meeting with the Chief Constable tomorrow morning," Andrew said as he walked Bessie to her door. "We're meeting in Ramsey, but I can come back and collect you before the meeting."

Bessie shook her head. "That's silly. You stay in Ramsey. I'm sure Doona or John or Hugh can bring me to the meeting. Or I can take a taxi. I'll see you there."

He protested a bit, but Bessie was able to convince him. After he'd done a quick check that everything was as it should be in Bessie's cottage, he headed for the door.

"I'm sorry to rush away, but I'm very tired tonight," he told her. "Travelling takes a lot out of me."

"Get some extra rest tonight, and I'll see you tomorrow," Bessie said, giving him a hug before she opened the door to let him out.

She watched, a frown on her face, as he slowly walked back to the nearest cottage. *He isn't doing as well as he claimed,* she thought, feeling worried about her dear friend.

"Hello," Doona said the next afternoon when Bessie opened the door to her knock. "Ready for our next cold case?"

Bessie shrugged. "Andrew said it's a really tough one this time."

"So maybe this will be the first one we don't solve. We can't expect to solve them all."

"But I want to solve them all."

Doona laughed. "Of course you do, but maybe that isn't realistic."

"I still want to do it."

The pair chatted and laughed together as Doona drove them to Ramsey. Bessie had never learned to drive. When she was younger, she'd relied on the island's buses and trains to get around, but, at some point, one of her friends had started a taxi service in Laxey. Because he knew Bessie well, he'd given her a generous discount, which meant his service quickly became her preferred way to travel.

Some years later, he'd sold the business to a company in Douglas, but they'd agreed to honour Bessie's discount if she continued to use their services. She had a standing appointment every Friday to do her grocery shopping, and during the weeks when Andrew was across, she used the service fairly regularly. When Andrew was on the island, though, he usually drove them both wherever they wanted to go.

Doona parked near the front of the building in the large car park at the Seaview Hotel.

"One day I'm going to get a room here, just for a night, just because," Doona said as they walked towards the entrance.

"It's such a beautiful old hotel," Bessie said as they walked into the huge lobby.

"There's my Aunt Bessie," Jasper Coventry, the hotel's owner and manager, said from behind the reception desk. He bustled out from behind the desk and pulled Bessie into a hug. "How are you?" he asked as the embrace ended.

"I'm fine. How are you?"

"I'm surprisingly good. Our chef and our pastry chef have been getting along together for several weeks now. I'm not sure why, but I'm grateful. Stuart has been less difficult than normal, too. I'm sure the moon is in retrograde or something, and it will all come crashing down soon, but for right now, I'm good."

Bessie laughed. "I didn't know you believed in such things."

Jasper shook his head. "I don't, but Stuart has been bored lately, so he's been reading his horoscope every day. He's been reading mine, too, but I won't let him tell me what it says. It keeps him amused and out of trouble, anyway."

Stuart was Jasper's partner. Bessie knew that he'd paid for a lot of the extensive renovation work that the pair had had done when they'd purchased the Seaview, but she wasn't sure how much of the work he did in connection with the day-to-day running of the property. Those responsibilities all seemed to fall on Jasper, but Bessie knew that Jasper loved his job.

"I've put you in the penthouse conference room today," Jasper said. "And now that our busy summer has died down to a slow autumnal trickle, I asked the chef and the pastry chef to put together a few treats for you, too."

"Lovely," Bessie said happily.

"I didn't get much lunch," Andrew said as he joined them.

"Then you'll enjoy the quiches," Jasper told him. "Chef has prepared three different quiches for you to enjoy today. There is a ham and cheese quiche. There is a six cheese and vegetable quiche. And there is a chicken and leek quiche."

"And now I'm sorry that I had lunch," Bessie said.

"I am, too," Doona said.

"Ah, but if you've eaten lunch, then you can enjoy pudding," Jasper told her. "Our pastry chef has prepared pies for today. You've been given an apple pie, a chocolate cream pie, and a strawberry and rhubarb pie. I suggest you try a small sliver of each."

"I may just have to do that," Bessie said, her mouth watering.

"I'm afraid I'm going to have to send you upstairs on your own. We're a bit short-handed here now that the summer rush is over. Sandra is back in school nearly every day, which means I'm covering the front desk most mornings," Jasper said.

"We can find the penthouse conference room," Bessie assured him.

"Enjoy. I hope the case is an easy one," Jasper called after them as they began to walk towards the lifts.

"I wish," Andrew sighed.

"We can only do our best," Bessie told him. "And even if we don't solve the case, maybe we can help move things in the right direction."

"Thank you. I needed that."

Inside the conference room with its gorgeous views of the sea below, Andrew filled a plate with slices of quiche while Bessie and Doona took small slivers of each of the pies. Then Bessie poured herself a cup of tea while Andrew and Doona got coffee. They were just taking their seats when the door opened and John and Hugh walked in.

"Jasper said there was all sorts of food," Hugh said happily.

"Help yourself after a proper hello," Bessie replied.

Hugh flushed and then stopped to greet everyone before rushing back to the table and filling a plate. He put the plate full of quiche at his place at the table and then went back and filled a second plate with pieces of pie. After getting himself a cup of tea, he took his seat and began to steadily work his way through the first plate of food.

"Why doesn't he get fat?" Doona asked Bessie.

"Because he still has the metabolism of a teenager," Bessie replied. To her, Hugh didn't look much older than fifteen, but the young man was married with a child and another on the way. After the many nights he'd spent in Bessie's spare room during his difficult teen years, though, she often thought that she'd never actually be able to think of him as a proper adult.

"I hope I'm not late," Charles said as he walked into the room.

John nodded at him from the back of the room where he was filling a plate. Charles walked back and looked at what was available. After a moment, he cut himself a small slice of apple pie and then poured himself a cup of coffee. He was just getting settled in his seat when the door opened again.

"Good afternoon," Harry said as he strode into the room. He glanced at the table in the back and then walked over and took a seat at the table, his back to the wall.

"Do you want coffee or tea?" John asked from where he was still standing near the table.

"I'm good," Harry replied.

John added one last slice of pie to his plate and then poured himself some tea. Then he crossed to the table and sat down next to Doona. She smiled at him as he picked up his fork.

"What do we have this time, then?" Harry asked Andrew.

Andrew sighed. "A case I'm already starting to regret agreeing to consider."

"Oh?" Charles said. "Why is that?"

"This one truly seems impossible," Andrew replied. "I know we've tackled a lot of difficult cases, but this one is difficult in every possible way."

"With all due respect," John said, "why are we considering it, then?"

"It was one of the first cases I was sent when I first set up the unit. I read through the summary and immediately dismissed it as too difficult. The thing is, though, it's been nagging at me ever since. Even though I only read a summary, I haven't been able to get the case out of my mind."

"That happens sometimes," Harry said.

23

"I think we all have unsolved cases we'll never forget," Charles muttered.

Andrew nodded. "After every case we've solved, I've reread the summary on this case. Finally, a few months ago, I rang Inspector Weaver, the lead investigator on the case. I told him that I didn't think we could do anything to help, but he didn't agree. He doesn't expect us to solve the case, but he's hopeful that we'll be able to help clarify at least a few things. He told me that he'll be happy if we can simply work out whom the killer was trying to kill."

"You've already lost me," Doona said.

Andrew nodded. "You'll probably be even more lost after you read the file." He opened his notebook and sighed. "Let me give you an overview of the case."

CHAPTER 3

Bessie pulled a small notebook out of her bag. While she would be getting a copy of the police file containing all of the information Andrew was about to share, she preferred to take notes when he gave them his summary of the case. Those notes helped her keep track of everyone as she read through the file.

"The story begins just a few days before Christmas, 1996," Andrew said.

"Five years ago," Charles muttered as he made a note.

Andrew nodded. "There was a Christmas party at a London luxury hotel. Invitations were sent to a long list of former guests. Those who chose to attend the party were given a special room rate for the weekend. That rate included the party and then breakfast the next morning."

"That sounds lovely," Doona said.

"A lot of people agreed with you," Andrew told her. "The hotel was filled to capacity, and every guest was there for the party."

"How many people?" Harry asked.

"Around a hundred. The hotel has fifty-seven rooms.

Most guests brought along a friend or family member. Rooms were limited to two guests each, and the party was strictly for adults only," Andrew replied.

"I remember hearing something about this," Harry said. "Wasn't there a problem with food poisoning or something?"

"That was how the story got reported in the papers, at least initially," Andrew told him. "Three people fell ill and died during the party, but it wasn't food poisoning. They were deliberately poisoned."

Harry nodded. "It's coming back to me now. I remember it being headline news for a few days, and then some minor royal got engaged on Christmas Day, or some cabinet minister got caught cheating, and the story more or less disappeared from the papers."

"It probably disappeared because there was no new information," Andrew said. "Scotland Yard put an entire team together to work the case, but they never got very far."

"I'm surprised you think we can do anything five years later," Charles said.

Andrew sighed. "I'm not sure we can, but I wanted to try."

Bessie frowned. "You said there were three victims. Were they all at the party together?"

Andrew shook his head. "They were all strangers to one another, at least as far as the police could determine."

"So one was the real target and the others were probably chosen at random," Harry said thoughtfully.

"Or someone just wanted to cause chaos and didn't care who died," John suggested.

Bessie shivered. "What a horrible thought."

"It is a horrible thought," Andrew agreed. "But it's one possibility. During the initial investigation, the police started with Harry's theory. They took a close look at the three victims and the person or persons who were at the party with them."

"But they never found the killer," John said.

"No, and over time Inspector Theodore Weaver, the lead investigator, has come to question just about everything that he and his team did during the investigation. He wants us to go back through the file and see what we conclude. I believe he's hoping that we'll agree with him and his approach to the investigation, but we may feel that he should have focused more of his energies in other areas."

"Tell us what happened at the party," Doona said.

"The party was held in the hotel's large conference area. It could be divided into smaller spaces, but for the party they used the entire room. There was a band and a small dance floor along one wall. There were bars set up along the other three walls."

"So they were expecting people to drink a lot," Charles said.

Andrew nodded. "The party included unlimited drinks, and, from what Theodore has told me, most of the guests took full advantage of that. Of course, that complicated things when it came time to question everyone."

John frowned. "Was the poison administered in food or drink?"

"Drink," Andrew replied. "It was in a bottle of white wine that was served to all three of the victims in fairly rapid succession. The first victim died within a minute of taking his first sip from his glass. The other two victims died shortly thereafter."

"And then no one else wanted white wine," Doona murmured.

Andrew nodded. "You can read the bartender's statement in the file. He reported that he'd opened the bottle, along with several others, as the first guests began to arrive. He said they always went through a lot of wine, both red and white, at those kinds of parties."

"What time did the party start?" Bessie asked.

"The party started at seven. The first victim died at three minutes past eight," Andrew told her.

"How many glasses of that particular wine did he pour before people started dying, then?" Harry asked.

"None," Andrew replied. "He said he'd been surprised, but that no one had requested that wine – it was a dry white wine – in the first hour of the evening. I should say that no one had requested that wine from *him*. His bar was in the corner farthest from the entrance, and it was the least busy of the three. In total, seventeen bottles of white wine were emptied during that first hour, and four of them were that particular dry white, but none of those bottles came from the bar at the back of the room."

"If that bar was so quiet, how did the killer manage to slip poison into one of the bottles?" Harry asked.

"That's one of the questions that the police could never answer," Andrew replied. "You can read about the poison in the report. Unfortunately, it was one that isn't terribly difficult to find, if you know where to look."

"What does that mean?" Bessie asked. "I thought poisons were carefully controlled and monitored."

Andrew shrugged. "Our government does its best, but it's also more diligent than governments in other parts of the world. The particular poison used in this case, though, is available in the UK. It has a variety of uses in cleaning and pest control. I suspect few people realise just how deadly it can be, but when used correctly it isn't any more dangerous than any other similar product."

"But the killer knew how to use it for his or her own aims," Charles said.

"Exactly. If you know where to look, the Internet has instructions on how to turn one of the most common household cleaners into a deadly poison," Andrew said.

"Surely that can't be legal," Doona said.

"The cleaner is legal. Turning it into poison is not," Andrew replied.

"So the bottle was sitting open for an entire hour before anyone ordered a glass," Charles said. "I hope we have pictures of the bar and the bottle."

"You do," Andrew assured him. "It wasn't a very big bar, and the bottles were on a table next to the bar so that the bartender could reach them easily. Theodore has done several reconstructions, and he's concluded that just about anyone could have walked up and tipped the poison into the bottle at any time during that hour. The bartender admitted that he was usually busy mixing drinks. He wasn't watching the bottles behind him in any way."

"Surely whoever did it would have wanted to make sure that his or her intended victim got a drink right away, though," Harry said. "The killer wouldn't have wanted to risk the bottle being emptied before the intended victim died."

"And from what you said, it sounds as if the poison was fast-acting," John added. "So the killer must have had to make sure that the victim got a drink as soon as the first glass from the bottle was poured. Otherwise, as soon as people started dying no one else would have had any white wine."

"Walk us through exactly what happened," Charles said.

Andrew opened his notebook and flipped through the pages. "I'm not going to give you any names yet. I'm just going to take you through the five minutes or so when everything happened."

"Five minutes?" Hugh repeated.

"It was actually more like four minutes," Andrew said. "At seven fifty-nine the first glass of wine from the poisoned bottle was poured. The person who ordered it was getting drinks for multiple people. As that person walked away, a second glass was requested. That person carried his drink to a nearby table while the third glass was being poured. The first victim was the second person to get a glass of wine. He'd walked back to the table where his girlfriend was waiting and then downed most of the contents of the glass. Victim two, who'd been the last to get a glass, was sipping wine as victim one fell to the ground."

Bessie looked up from her notes. "Were they both still standing near the bar?"

Andrew nodded. "They'd moved a short distance away, but not far. The first person, though, who'd ordered the wine for someone else, was on the other side of the room as the first victim collapsed. Without realizing what was happening, the third victim started drinking the wine as people started shouting near the bar."

"So if one of the victims was the intended victim, the killer had to have moved fast," Doona said. "He or she had to get the intended victim to drink the wine before the victim realized what was happening."

"How long did it take for someone to realise that the poison was in the wine?" Harry asked.

"Not long," Andrew replied. "One of the guests at the party was a retired senior policeman. As soon as the second victim collapsed, he started shouting at everyone to stop eating and drinking. Unfortunately, he was just a few seconds too late to save the third victim, but he did prevent things from getting worse."

"It seems a very inefficient way of murdering someone," Bessie said.

"Indeed," Andrew said. "And yet three people died, and the killer has evaded detection for five years."

"We have to question whether the killer accomplished his or her aim, though," Charles said. "It seems possible, maybe even likely, that things happened too quickly, leaving the killer's intended victim alive and well."

Andrew nodded. "That's one of the things that Theodore wants us to consider."

"I'm not sure how we do that," John said. "Between guests and hotel staff, there were over a hundred people there. Any one of them could have gone there planning to murder someone else."

"And we have to consider the possibility that the killer simply wanted to kill," Harry said in a low voice. "For the thrill of it, or to make some sort of statement, or maybe because he or she wanted to cause damage to the hotel, or for some other reason we can't even fathom."

"I hope that isn't the case," Bessie said. "It's bad enough thinking that someone deliberately killed a friend or a family member. Killing just to kill is even more horrible."

"I will say that no terrorist organisation has ever claimed responsibility," Andrew said.

"So where do we start?" Doona asked.

"With the case files." Andrew pulled a huge stack of envelopes out of his briefcase. "As you can imagine, there are thousands and thousands of pages of interviews from everyone who was at the party that evening. There's no way everyone here can go through all of the reports for this case. We're going to have to divide up the labour this time."

"But I want to read it all," Bessie protested as a few of the others looked surprised.

"I know you do. I'm sure you all do, but this is the full report." Andrew held up a thick stack of papers, "What I've done is copy the report twice and then divide it into sections. There were forty-three members of staff working in the hotel that evening. That includes everyone from the housekeeping staff, who weren't supposed to be anywhere near the party, to the bartenders, waitresses, and managers on duty. Then there were around a hundred guests."

"That would be a lot of statements to read," Charles said.

"There are three sections. Two sections of party guests, with about fifty statements in each section, and one section of employees, with forty-three statements in it. I've pulled out the statements from the people with connections to the victims. I want everyone to read those reports, of course."

"So who gets which sections, and what are we supposed to do with them?" Doona asked.

"I'll answer your second question first. I want you to work in pairs, reading through your section of statements and looking for anything that might have been missed the first time. We're looking for hints that someone else was the intended victim or anything else that feels wrong in any way. I want to work through that before we look at the victims and their companions."

"Does that mean you aren't going to tell us anything about them today?" Bessie asked.

Andrew hesitated and then shook his head. "I'll tell you their names and a few brief facts about each of them, because every suspect was asked about his or her relationship with each of the victims. I'm not going to give you any more than that for now, though. Tomorrow, you'll get the statements from the people who were at the party with the victims."

"If we're meeting again tomorrow, that only gives us tonight to work through our fifty or so statements," Doona said.

"Does that not give you enough time?" Andrew asked.

"I suppose that depends on who I'm working with," Doona replied.

"I thought you could work with John," Andrew told her.

Doona smiled at John. "We didn't have anything better to do tonight, did we?" she asked.

He chuckled. "I was planning on spending the night going through the new case file."

"Yeah, me, too," Doona said with a wry smile.

"I'm going to give you half of the party guests," Andrew said, passing Doona a thick stack of papers. "There are copies for each of you."

Doona flipped through the sheets and then sighed. "I'm going to have to make a lot of coffee," she said as she slipped the pile of paperwork into the large bag she'd brought with her.

"Charles and Harry, I thought you two could work together, since you're both staying at the Seaview," Andrew said.

Both men nodded.

Andrew passed Harry another thick stack of papers. "Those are the statements from the staff," he told them.

"These should make for interesting reading," Harry said.

"The first ten, anyway," Charles said. "I suspect they might get a bit repetitive after that."

"That just leaves us," Hugh said to Bessie. "And I suppose we get the other fifty party guests."

"You do," Andrew agreed. He handed Bessie her stack of papers. "I hope you two can find time to go through these together."

"I need to go home and check on Grace," Hugh said. "But assuming she's not too tired from running after Aalish all day, I'll come over to your cottage right after dinner."

Bessie nodded. "That sounds good. We can read through the statements over tea and biscuits."

"Great," Hugh said, beaming.

"But that doesn't leave you anything to do," Harry said to Andrew.

He grinned. "I've already read through the entire file. I'm going to take tonight off." As everyone looked surprised, he laughed. "I'm not really taking the night off. I'm going to go back through everything and pull out the statements from the people I thought might warrant a bit

33

of extra attention. We'll see tomorrow if you all agree with my assessments."

"What about the victims, then?" Harry asked, turning to a new page in his notebook.

"The first victim was a man called Dennis Baker. He was fifty when he died," Andrew told them.

Bessie took notes. "Whom was he with at the party?" she asked.

"His girlfriend, Naomi Farmer. She was twenty-seven at the time."

"That's quite an age gap," Doona said.

Andrew nodded. "Dennis was a successful businessman with a reputation as something of a playboy. From what Theodore was able to discover, his relationships rarely lasted for much longer than six months."

"Is there a motive for murder there?" Harry asked.

Andrew shrugged. "Theodore's team spoke to a number of his former girlfriends. They were fairly unanimous in stating that Dennis had broken their hearts, but they also all reported that he'd given them very generous gifts when ending the relationships."

"How long had he been seeing Naomi?" Doona asked.

"About three months," Andrew said. "And from all accounts, they were happy together."

Bessie frowned. "Maybe someone else at the party had a motive for murdering Dennis."

"Maybe, but if so, Theodore couldn't find the connection," Andrew told her. "And that's all I'm going say about Dennis for today. The second victim was Laurence Lawrence."

"Why would his parents do that?" Hugh asked.

"He was named after his father's closest friend from uni," Andrew told him. "Apparently his mother objected, but his father won in the end."

"Poor guy," Hugh said.

"Tell us about Laurence, then," Harry said.

Andrew spent a moment looking at his notes before looking back up. "He was thirty and engaged to be married. He'd come to the party with his fiancée, June Allison. Multiple people at the party reported that they'd heard the pair arguing throughout the evening, but no one seemed to think that the argument was anything serious, at least not before Laurence dropped dead."

"What were they fighting about?" Doona asked.

"No one seemed entirely certain, and after the murder June insisted that they weren't fighting at all. You'll be able to read about it in some of the statements," Andrew replied.

Doona made a note and then frowned at her notebook.

"And the final victim?" Bessie asked.

"Was the person who got the first glass of wine from the bottle," Andrew replied. "Brenda Morgan was forty-five, and she was at the party with her sister, Myra, and two other friends, who were staying in the room next door to theirs."

"Had they also been invited to the party?" Doona asked.

Andrew nodded. "Anyone who'd been a guest at the hotel throughout the year was invited. Brenda and her friends, Lucy Dawson and Olga Chandler, had stayed at the hotel in July, celebrating a friend's engagement."

"What friend?" Bessie wondered.

"A friend who is irrelevant to the case," Andrew told her. "While Brenda, Myra, Lucy, and Olga were in London at the Christmas party, the friend was on her honeymoon in Mallorca."

"So Brenda was friends with the other two women. Was her sister also part of the same social circle?" Doona asked.

Andrew shook his head. "According to Myra, she and her sister had drifted apart during her marriage, but the trip to London was partly in celebration of Myra's divorce. Myra told Theodore that she'd been hoping that she and Brenda would be a lot closer now that her ex-husband was out of the picture."

"I don't suppose he was in London the night of the party," Harry said.

"Unfortunately, he was not," Andrew said. "He was in Guernsey, where they were all living at the time."

"I suppose none of the guests actually lived in London, did they?" Doona asked. "I mean, if they did, they didn't have any reason to stay in a hotel there."

"They might have, if they wanted a night out and didn't want to worry about driving after drinking," Harry said.

Andrew nodded. "When you read through the various statements, you'll find that some of the guests did live in London. Most of them, however, were from elsewhere."

"And none of them knew one another," Bessie said thoughtfully. "Or so they claimed."

"Theodore spent a lot of time and effort trying to find links between the victims and between the victims and the other guests. Aside from a few tenuous links that are all discussed in the file, he was unsuccessful."

"Define tenuous," Harry said.

Andrew grinned. "A few of the guests had bank accounts in Guernsey, but none of those guests had ever actually been to Guernsey. They were simply keeping some of their money offshore for the tax advantages. One of the other guests was once flatmates with someone who'd gone out with Dennis Baker, but the women had stopped living together some years before the friend met Dennis. They also only went out twice. There are a few other, similar stories."

Harry frowned. "Tenuous was a good word for them."

"I think we'll stop there for today," Andrew said, glancing at the clock on the wall. "Does anyone have any questions?"

"If we finish our assigned group early, can we have more?" Bessie asked.

Andrew shook his head. "For tonight, focus on the section you've been given. We'll talk tomorrow about how we move forwards. I'm here for a fortnight, and this time we might need every minute of it to make any progress."

Harry frowned. "Charles and I are supposed to fly home in a week. Should we change our flights and see if the hotel can extend our stay?"

"That's up to you," Andrew replied. "Maybe leave it for a few days and see how much progress we make in that time."

"Maybe we'll solve it tomorrow," Doona said.

A few people chuckled.

"I can't see that happening, but I'd be delighted if we did," Andrew said as everyone started to get up from their chairs. "I'll see you all back here at the same time tomorrow," he added as Harry and Charles headed for the door.

CHAPTER 4

"I can see why you were hesitant to take on this case," Bessie said as Andrew drove them back to Laxey.

He sighed. "I'm still not sure I made the right decision. We have one hundred and fifty or so suspects to consider, and we've no idea whom the killer was targeting, or if anyone was actually being targeted."

"I'm intrigued, but not optimistic," Bessie said. "I remember reading something about the case when it happened. It wasn't all that long ago. I can't quite believe that I'm being given access to the police reports for the case."

"Don't get too excited. There's very little information in them that isn't public knowledge. And I don't know that anything in the file is going to help us, anyway."

"We'll just have to do our best."

"And so far, that's been good enough to solve every case. I don't know that it will make much difference this time."

"I suppose we'll just have to wait and see."

Andrew glanced over at Bessie and grinned. "You're still

just the tiniest bit optimistic that we're going to solve the case, aren't you?"

She smiled back. "Maybe a bit more than the tiniest bit."

He pulled the car into the parking area outside of her cottage and switched off the engine. "I think I could do with a walk on the beach. My head is pounding."

"Let me put my paperwork in the cottage and then I'll join you," Bessie said.

Inside, she carried the paperwork up to her office and locked it in a drawer. Then she changed into shoes more suited for walking on the sand and headed back outside. She and Andrew walked for several minutes in silence.

"I think my biggest worry is that our perfect record is going to be spoiled," Andrew said eventually.

"It's going to happen sooner or later," Bessie said. "We all know we can't solve every single case. At least this one feels impossible from the outset."

He shrugged. "Have I told you that my grandson is going back to school?"

"You haven't. Which grandson, and what does he want to study?"

The pair chatted about various members of Andrew's family as they strolled as far as Thie yn Traie and then walked slowly back towards Bessie's cottage.

"Helen wanted me to invite you to dinner tonight," Andrew said when they reached his cottage. "She's going to start cooking once she's finished with work for the day."

"If you're certain she wants guests, I'd love to come to dinner."

"I know she wants guests. We're both getting quite tired of one another. We've been spending far more time together than either of us is used to, and we're running out of things about which to talk."

39

Bessie laughed. "What time do you want me to come over?"

"Helen was planning dinner for six. Does that work for you?"

"I'm sure it will. Hugh and I are meeting after dinner, which I assume means seven or later. I'll text him and let him know where to find me if he's ready to start working earlier, though."

"And now I think I might take a short nap," Andrew said, stopping in front of Bessie's door. "I'll see you later."

She gave him a hug and then watched as he walked back to his own cottage. To Bessie's mind, they'd walked fairly slowly up and down the beach, but Andrew made his way back to his rental cottage at an even slower pace. Frowning, Bessie let herself into Treoghe Bwaane and shut the door behind herself. Worry about Andrew filled her thoughts as she slipped off her shoes and hung up her jacket. When the phone rang, she reached for it without thinking.

"Hello?"

"Bessie? Hello."

"Hello," Bessie replied, suspicious that the caller was about to try to sell her something.

"How are you?"

"I'm fine, thank you. How are you?"

"Quite dreadful, really, and I didn't know who else to ring."

"I'm very sorry to hear that," Bessie said. *But who is this?* she wondered.

"I hate to bother you, though, especially now that the whole island knows that you're working on that cold case unit."

"It does keep me rather busy."

"Aye, I'm sure it does, but I didn't know who else to ring."

"What's wrong?"

"Maybe nothing, but I just don't know for certain."

Bessie took a deep breath. "You're going to have to tell me more than that."

"I'm sorry. I'm making a right mess of this. I planned everything I was going to say. I even took notes so I'd do it all in the right order. But now that I'm actually talking to you, I'm just making a mess."

"Let's start at the beginning. Who is this?"

The other woman laughed shakily. "I even missed that bit, did I? It's Marion, er, Marion Crellin."

"From Lonan?" Bessie asked. On a small island with a handful of common surnames and a small variety of popular Christian names, Bessie needed to be sure which Marion Crellin had rung.

"Aye, yes, that Marion Crellin," the other woman replied. "I know we haven't spoken in years, but I still remember playing on Laxey Beach as a child. Your cottage seemed an almost magical place, full of biscuits and cakes. My mum said you made the best tea on the island."

Bessie laughed. "I don't think it was anything special."

"But your cottage was a respite from, well, everything. My father didn't treat Mum very well, which you probably knew."

Bessie frowned. "I didn't know anything for certain, but I had my suspicions."

"Mum said she always felt stronger after she'd spent some time with you. Silvester and I just enjoyed the biscuits."

"How is your brother?"

"Ah, but that's why I rang. He's disappeared."

"Oh, no."

Marion took a deep breath. "Let me do this right," she said. "You know that he moved across after Mum died, right?"

"I did hear that. That was fifteen years ago or more."

"It was. Dad died when I was eighteen. Mum was devastated, in spite of everything, but eventually she came to realise that she was much better off without him. As you said, we lost her sixteen years ago."

"And then Silvester moved across?"

"Aye, he'd always wanted to go, but he'd never wanted to leave Mum. Once she was gone, I told him that he could go if he still wanted to. I didn't want him staying here just for my benefit, even though I miss him terribly."

"Where did he go?"

"Just to Liverpool. He wanted to be able to get back to the island regularly and he doesn't like to fly, so Liverpool suits him. Whenever he wants to come home, he can jump on the ferry and be here in a few hours."

"And does he like living in Liverpool?"

"Oh, aye, mostly, anyway. It's a big city. Silvester always loved big cities. I don't mind visiting them, but I wouldn't want to live in one."

"Me neither."

"Anyway, he moved across and got a job as a waiter in one of the restaurants near the docks. He got a flat near there, too."

"Wasn't he cooking in one of the island hotels before he left?"

"He was, aye, but he couldn't find work cooking over there when he first arrived. It didn't take him long to move up, though. He's an assistant chef at a nice hotel over there now – or he was, before he disappeared."

"Good for him."

"Yeah, well, if he'd quit drinking, he could do a lot more, but you know Silvester."

Bessie sighed. "He's still drinking too much, then?"

"Oh, aye, but only on nights when he isn't working. He tells me all the time that he's very careful and that he never drinks when he has to work the next day. The last time I visited, the head chef told me the same thing, actually, but I still think he'd be better off if he quit."

"But now he's missing?"

"He is," Marion said, clearly upset.

"When did you last speak to him?"

"On Saturday. Weekends are busy for the hotel, so we don't usually talk on Saturdays, but he rang me on Saturday night. He said he had a surprise for me and that I should get ready to meet someone special."

"Someone special?"

Marion sighed. "I assumed he's thinking of getting married again."

"How many times has he been married?"

"Four, although I'm not sure all of the marriages were legal. I'm not sure about the divorces, either. And that's what I said to Silvester when he rang. I said, 'Are you sure you're divorced from the last mistake?' He just laughed and then said he'd ring me again soon."

"And you haven't heard from him since?"

"No, and I know it's only Tuesday, but the thing is, yesterday was my birthday. Silvester has his faults, but, in all of my sixty-two years, he's never missed my birthday, not once."

"Happy birthday," Bessie said.

Marion snorted. "It isn't though, not with my brother missing."

"I assume you've tried ringing him."

"Of course I've tried ringing him. I rang on Sunday afternoon because we usually talk on Sunday afternoons, but he didn't answer. I left a message on his answering machine and assumed he'd ring me on my birthday. But then he didn't. By the end of the day yesterday, I was starting to get worried, so I rang again. No one answered.

Then I rang this morning and again this afternoon. Nothing."

"What about ringing his work or a neighbour?"

"I tried ringing the hotel. The head chef told me that Silvester has taken a few days off and isn't expected back until Friday. Usually, when he takes time off, he comes back to the island."

"Maybe he took time off to be with the new person in his life."

"Maybe, but that doesn't explain why he isn't answering his phone."

"I assume he has a mobile phone."

"Yeah, and he isn't answering that, either. I never ring that number, because he usually has it switched off, but I did try it on Monday night and again today. It's switched off."

"I think you should ring the police and file a missing person report."

Marion sighed. "I don't want to upset Silvester. What if he's off having a romantic time with his new girlfriend and then the police turn up? He'd never forgive me."

"He should have told you if he was going away with his girlfriend."

"I know, but maybe it was a last-minute thing. And maybe he just forgot about my birthday."

"I'm not sure what you want me to do," Bessie said after a moment.

"You know all about finding missing people. I thought maybe you could help me find him."

"I don't know that much about finding missing people, and, even if I did, I still think you need to ring the police."

"Can't you at least suggest a few things I could do?"

Bessie thought for a minute. "The police would start by ringing the local hospital and seeing if anyone had been brought in matching your brother's description," she said hesitantly.

"I already tried that," Marion told her. "I rang the Liverpool newspaper, too, and asked if there were any unidentified dead bodies that might be Silvester. They said no."

"That's good news."

"It is, but it doesn't get us any closer to finding Silvester."

"What do you know about the woman in his life?"

"Nothing. I don't even know for sure that there is a woman in his life. I'm just guessing that was what he was hinting at when we last spoke."

"What about previous girlfriends?"

"His last serious relationship was his last marriage. That ended while he was still living on the island. He told me after they split up that he was never getting involved with anyone again."

"So he's been single for a long time."

"A lot longer than I expected, really. He's never happier than when he has someone new in his life. Sadly, once the initial infatuation wears off, he gets bored really quickly. None of his marriages lasted longer than a year."

"But he's been in Liverpool for the last fifteen years. Maybe he's been involved with several women during those years."

"Not Silvester. If he was seeing anyone, he would have told me. He tells me all about everything that happens in his life."

"But he'd never mentioned this woman to you before?"

"No, which means they had to have just started seeing one another recently. He might have gone out with her once or twice without telling me, but not more than that."

"Did you ask anyone at his work about any women in his life?"

"No, but I should have. I just rang and asked for Silvester.

When they told me that he was on holiday for a few days, I was so surprised that I just put the phone down."

"Maybe you should try ringing them again," Bessie suggested.

Marion sighed. "I can try. What else can I do?"

"You can file a missing person report."

"Not yet. He hasn't been missing for long. If it hadn't been my birthday yesterday, I probably wouldn't have worried until next Sunday, when we were due to talk again. We miss speaking now and again and I've never worried about it until now."

"I'm afraid I don't know what else to suggest."

"I'll ring the hotel again and see if I can find out more about Silvester's girlfriend." There was a long pause before Marion spoke again. "I don't suppose you'd be willing to ring them on my behalf? After all the investigations you've been involved in, you'll have a much better idea of what to ask."

"I can't imagine anyone there would be willing to answer my questions. I'm a complete stranger to them all."

"I can ring and tell them that you'll be ringing," Marion suggested. "That's probably for the best. I'll ring and talk to Eugene. He's the restaurant's manager. I'll tell him that I'm worried about Silvester and let him know that I'm having a trained investigator look into his disappearance. Then you can ring and talk to him."

"I'm hardly a trained investigator," Bessie protested.

"You're part of an official Scotland Yard cold case unit. That's pretty impressive, if you ask me."

"I am part of the unit, but the police are much better positioned to find your brother."

"But you will help anyway, won't you?" Marion asked. "It's just one quick conversation with Eugene, who is very nice, by the way. He probably doesn't know anything."

"If he doesn't know anything, will you file a police report?"

"Let's see what Eugene says first," Marion said. "I'll ring him around ten tomorrow morning. I can't ring now. It's nearly time for the dinner crowd, but the restaurant should be fairly quiet tomorrow morning. I'll tell him that you're going to ring at half ten. Let me give you the number."

Bessie frowned as she picked up the pen next to the telephone. Marion read out a number, and Bessie carefully wrote it down and then repeated it back to Marion.

"That's it," Marion said. "Thank you so much."

"I'll ring you after I talk to Eugene," Bessie told her. "Ring me back if you hear from Silvester between now and then."

"Oh, I hope I do," Marion said. "I'm trying so hard not to worry."

Bessie put the receiver down and then sighed. As if she didn't have enough to worry about, now she was concerned about Marion and Silvester.

"And look at the time," she muttered as she got up from her chair. "It's almost time to meet Andrew and Helen for dinner, and you haven't done a single thing except talk to Marion."

There seemed no point in starting to go through the case file, not when she was supposed to work on it with Hugh, so Bessie did some tidying and vacuumed the ground floor. Living right on the beach meant that sand seemed to get everywhere in the cottage, no matter how often Bessie vacuumed. That job out of the way, for the day anyway, Bessie went upstairs and combed her hair. After adding a coat of lipstick and a bit of powder to her face, she went back down and pulled on her shoes and jacket. A minute later, she knocked on the door to Andrew's cottage.

"Good evening," Helen said as she pulled Bessie into a hug.

Bessie thought the world of Andrew's daughter. Because of Andrew's health concerns, his doctor wanted him to have someone with him at all times. Bessie was grateful that Helen was able to make the journey to the island most months so that the cold case unit could continue to meet there. While Bessie was willing to travel to London for meetings if necessary, she very much preferred to have them on the island.

"How was your day?" Bessie asked as the woman led her into the cottage.

"It was good. I got a lot done, actually, so I may be able to take the afternoon off on Friday. We'll have to see how the rest of the week goes, of course."

Andrew joined them a moment later. The trio talked about Helen's job and the island's weather while they enjoyed the steak and kidney pie that Helen had prepared.

"I made jam roly-poly for pudding," Helen said as she cleared away the dinner dishes. "And I have custard."

"Wonderful," Bessie said.

Andrew grinned. "I never realised how much better it would be if Helen travelled with me."

After pudding, Andrew walked Bessie back to her cottage. They were still chatting on her doorstep when Hugh pulled into the parking area. He parked and then jumped out of the car and walked briskly over to Bessie.

"I'm really eager to get started," he said. "I have a good feeling about this case, even though I know I shouldn't."

"Come in and we can get started, then," Bessie said.

Andrew gave her a hug before he turned and walked back towards his cottage. Bessie watched him go for a moment before shaking her head and then walking inside. Hugh followed.

CHAPTER 5

"Is Andrew okay?" Hugh asked as Bessie filled the kettle.

"I think so," Bessie replied. "You know he has some health concerns. I believe he's going to be having surgery in the new year."

"Something else to worry about, then," Hugh said in a low voice.

"What else is wrong?" Bessie asked, concerned about her young friend.

"Nothing really, except Grace and I are both worried about bringing the new baby home. We don't want to upset Aalish, who is used to having our undivided attention."

"I'm sure it will be strange for her, but she's getting a sibling, and siblings are wonderful blessings."

"And she may come to appreciate the baby one day, but I suspect the first few months are going to be incredibly hard for all of us."

"Not least because you and Grace won't be getting enough sleep."

Hugh groaned and then sank into a chair. "I keep telling myself that it will be easier this time around, that Grace and I will do a better job of managing the sleepless nights, but I'm not sure that's true. And it isn't as if Aalish sleeps through the night every night anyway. Between her and the new baby, I may not get to sleep ever again."

Bessie chuckled and then patted his back. "I promise, you will get to sleep again, but you should be getting as much extra sleep now as you possibly can. And spare some sympathy for your lovely wife, who probably can't get comfortable enough to get extra sleep."

"She is already struggling to find a comfortable position in bed, and even when she does get comfortable for a little while, she isn't comfortable for long. I keep reminding her that she's growing a baby, which is just amazing, but she is pretty grumpy about the whole thing a lot of the time."

Bessie laughed. "I don't blame her. I can't imagine what she's going through. Remind her that she's always welcome here for a change of scenery. I reckon I could entertain Aalish for an hour or two if Grace wanted a nap one day."

"I'll tell her. She might be more interested in napping in your spare room once the baby arrives, but I don't think you want to look after Aalish and a new baby."

"I'm afraid I have very little idea of what to do with a baby. I've next to no experience with them."

Hugh grinned. "You're excellent with teenagers, though. I can't imagine Aalish as a teenager, but I suppose it will happen one day."

"And before you know it. Enjoy her toddler years. They truly will fly past."

Bessie had piled biscuits onto a plate and put it on the table while they'd been talking. She'd added small plates for each of them and had then taken out teacups. As the kettle boiled, she prepared the tea.

THE LAWRENCE FILE

As she put the teacups on the table, Hugh smiled. "Thank you," he said. "I'm ready to focus on the case now."

"That's good to hear. I'm not sure that I am, though. It all seems rather pointless. I can't imagine that we're going to be able to solve it."

"As I said earlier, I'm oddly optimistic about this case. Maybe it's just because we've solved all of the others. I have faith that Andrew knows how to select cases that are solvable."

Bessie picked up her fat envelope and sighed. "All of this and we only have a third of the suspects here."

"But once we get through them, we can get the statements that really matter – the ones from the people who were at the party with the victims."

"You're assuming that one of the victims was actually the intended target."

Hugh nodded. "Because that makes the most sense, and I can't see us solving the case otherwise." He pulled open his envelope and extracted the file folder from inside it as Bessie did the same.

"Andrew didn't say anything about pictures," Bessie said in surprise as she opened her folder.

"Pictures?" Hugh opened his folder and stared at the first picture inside it. "Wow, that's a lot of people."

Bessie sighed. "They're all dressed for a party, but they all look scared and sad." She flipped through the small pile of photos.

"I assume you have the same six pictures that I have," Hugh said after a minute. "Three of the crowd, each taken from a different angle, and then one of each victim."

Bessie nodded. "There's a note under the last picture. Apparently, these were taken by the retired senior policeman who was a guest at the party. He used his personal camera to capture what he could in the seconds after the victims died. I gather we'll get the official crime scene photos later."

"Does it matter where people are standing?" Hugh asked as he studied one of the pictures. "I mean, some of these people are quite far from where the victims are lying. Does that mean they're too far away to have put the poison in the wine bottle?"

"I wish I knew," Bessie said with a shrug. "It's difficult for me to imagine how someone managed to put the poison in the bottle and then make sure that the person he or she wanted to kill actually drank it."

"Maybe that wasn't what happened," Hugh said. "Maybe the killer dumped the poison in the bottle after getting the drink for the victim. Maybe he or she added poison to the victim's glass separately."

"But that still means he or she poured poison into a bottle that was behind a bar in one corner of the room. I can't imagine that any of the guests had access to that bottle."

Hugh looked back down at the file. "There's a rough floor plan. The bar that served the poisoned drinks was at the back of the room."

Bessie studied the floor plan and then looked at the pictures again. "It looks as if the tables with food were right next to that bar," she said as she worked her way through them. "Presumably nearly everyone got something to eat during the evening."

"There are more pictures," Hugh said as he worked his way down the stack of papers in his folder. "And this makes it all a bit clearer."

Bessie found the pictures he'd located. These had been taken of the room when it was empty. There were a few close-up photos of the bar where the fatal drinks had been served. A red "X" marked the spot where the open wine bottle had been sitting during the evening.

"Anyone could have added something to that bottle while getting food," Hugh said with a sigh.

"That bottle or a dozen others," Bessie added. "They were all just sitting there, right next to the tables where the food was set out."

Hugh looked up from the notes on the sheet after the pictures. "According to this, the wine bottles had been opened and then the corks had been replaced loosely to help keep the wine fresh. They opened six bottles of wine at every bar before the door opened, in anticipation of the initial rush."

Bessie looked through the pictures again. "We have to assume that everyone in the room had the opportunity to poison the wine," she said eventually.

Hugh nodded. "But once the poison was in there, the killer had to act fast. He or she had to get the victim to drink the wine before anyone realised what was happening."

"And it seems possible that he or she failed," Bessie said. "We have to consider that every person at the party may have been the intended victim and may be the killer."

"I hope the police asked everyone what they were drinking. The intended victim had to prefer dry white wine, right?"

Bessie thought for a minute. "I suppose so," she said eventually. "Unless the killing truly was simply random."

Hugh sighed. "There are too many possibilities."

"And we haven't even started reading the witness statements yet."

"Let's work through the first ten or so of those and then talk again," Hugh suggested.

Bessie nodded and then got out her notebook. While taking notes on fifty different people seemed a daunting task, she always took notes while she read statements.

"Should we both read the same ones, or should I start at the end and work backwards?" Hugh asked.

"Let's try reading the same ones for this first batch. We can always change it up later, after we've gone through the first ten."

An hour later, Bessie's head hurt and her hand was cramped. She'd taken extensive notes on the first few witnesses, but it had quickly become obvious to her that she was wasting her time. As Hugh put down his pen and sat back with a sigh, she got to her feet.

"Headache tablets?" she asked.

Hugh nodded. "Yes, please."

Neither of them spoke as Bessie made them more tea and refilled the plate of biscuits, which was mostly empty. While Bessie didn't remember eating any of the sweet treats, her small plate was dotted with crumbs.

"So, that was hard work," Hugh said. "And it felt pretty futile, too. No one saw anything. No one knew any of the victims. Everyone was just having fun, celebrating Christmas, right up until the first victim fell to the ground."

"And they all dearly loved their friend or family member who was with them at the party," Bessie added.

"And only one of the ten regularly drank wine – but red, not white."

"Which means he was probably not the intended victim, and neither were any of the other nine."

"We have forty more to go."

"I shouldn't need as long with the rest now that I've stopped taking lengthy notes," Bessie said. "Let's try to get through the next ten in only half an hour."

"Do you have any specific comments on any of the first ten?"

"I wish I did, but I don't."

"Me neither. Round Two," Hugh said, tapping his teacup to make a ringing sound.

Twenty-eight minutes later, Bessie sat back in her chair. Hugh was already sitting up, munching his way through a biscuit.

"We are getting faster," Hugh said.

"Only because we aren't learning anything. This lot was the same as the first batch. No one knew anything."

"There was one dry white wine drinker. I took notes on her."

"Agnes Jacobs," Bessie said. "A seventy-two-year-old widow who was at the party with her sister's only child, Michael Davidson."

"I read Michael's statement twice, but I couldn't find anything in it to suggest that he had any reason to want his Aunt Agnes dead."

"He'd invited her to the party as a special treat for her. He did admit that he was probably her heir, but, as he pointed out, he's considerably better off than she is. They both said that they'd always had a special relationship because Agnes had never had children of her own."

"We have to consider her as a possible victim, but I think it's unlikely."

Bessie nodded. "And that was the only interesting thing in that entire group."

"Half an hour for the next group?"

"Let's try to get through them faster."

"Done," Hugh shouted happily twenty-four minutes later.

Bessie finished reading the last sheet in the pile and sighed. "I can't help but feel as if we're wasting our time."

"But George thought he saw something. He was on the opposite side of the room, and he was a little bit drunk, but he was certain he saw someone pour something into one of the bottles behind the bar."

Bessie sighed. "I don't really think that George is a very sound witness, but even if we believe everything he said, it doesn't help in the slightest. He couldn't tell the police anything about the person he thought he saw."

"We did find someone else who was drinking dry white wine."

"We did, but she and her husband were newlyweds who'd come to the party together. I'd hate to think that he was trying to kill her."

"They both sounded as if they were happily married."

"Let's work on the next ten and then take a tea break," Bessie suggested.

Hugh nodded. "That sounds good. Half an hour or less."

It took Hugh thirty-five minutes to get through the next ten. Bessie was a few minutes behind him.

"So, Albert Stone," Hugh said as Bessie put her pen down.

"Exactly," she said. "He was drinking dry white wine."

"And he and his companion weren't getting along very well."

"He and Harold North were business partners," Bessie said, reading from her notes. "They'd been partners for almost thirty years, and they both agreed that they had been fighting more and more every year since they'd first met."

"And they had insurance policies on each other's lives."

Bessie put her pen down and sat back in her chair. "I didn't care for Harold. He came across as a very unpleasant person when he was interviewed."

"He complained a lot about the amount of time it took the police to interview everyone. He also seemed quite annoyed that the party had been interrupted."

"I got the feeling that he thought the police should have removed the bodies and then allowed the party to continue."

Hugh chuckled. "He was quite unhappy that he hadn't

THE LAWRENCE FILE

been allowed to get more to drink while he'd been waiting for his turn to speak to the police."

"Maybe he was unhappy because his plan to kill his business partner had failed."

"Maybe. I think the police should take another look at him. I'm especially interested in knowing what he's been doing since the murders."

"I'm a bit worried about Albert, actually. If Harold wasn't behind the murders, I'm afraid they might have put ideas into his head."

"The other eight people were quite dull."

"Some of them are probably very interesting people, but for our purposes, I suppose it helps when they're dull. We can tentatively eliminate them from consideration."

"Only ten more to go."

"And I need more tea before I look at them."

Bessie made tea while Hugh refilled the biscuit plate. Then they both sat down with their last ten interviews. Twenty-three minutes later, Hugh was done. Bessie wasn't far behind.

"I'm going to be honest and say that I may not have given this group as much attention as I gave the first group," Hugh said.

"I tried, but my eyes are glazing over," Bessie admitted. "There wasn't anything interesting in any of these interviews, though."

"So where are we?" Hugh asked.

"I don't know that we're anywhere. We've read what fifty people had to say about the evening. None of them saw anything, aside from George, um…" She checked her notes. "George Hartman. He thinks he might have seen something but couldn't answer any questions about what he thinks he saw."

"According to the notes with the pictures, the lights were low and there were fairy lights everywhere. That would have cast all sorts of odd shadows. It seems possible that someone could have been watching the killer the entire time and still not seen the poison being added to the bottle."

Bessie nodded. "It was dark. There were a lot of people moving around the room. The bar was right next to the food, which means just about everyone walked past the bottle at some point during the first hour of the party."

"There were a few people who denied going anywhere near the bar at the back of the room."

"But none of them could prove that they hadn't gone back there. A few of them admitted to getting food, which means they were near the bar, even if they didn't get a drink from it. Others claimed they didn't get anything to eat or visit that bar, but no one had any way to prove it."

"For now, they are all suspects."

"But the ones who were at the party with people drinking dry white wine have to be higher on the list than the rest."

"I agree. Which brings us back to Albert Stone and Harold North."

"Out of the fifty statements, they were the only two that I think merit a closer look," Bessie said.

"Let's hope the others have had better luck with their sections."

"Charles and Harry got the employees. I'd like to read the statement from the bartender who served the poisoned drinks."

Hugh nodded. "I'm sure we'll get to read it eventually. I'm really too tired tonight to do it justice, though. Andrew was right. Fifty statements is just about all my brain can handle in a single evening."

"I hate to admit it, but I agree. I'm exhausted and frustrated. That doesn't mean I don't want to read all of the other statements, though. I'll just have to work through them slowly."

"I feel as if we might still be working on this case when it comes time to start the next one."

"If we can't solve it, I don't intend to stop working on it."

"Yeah, that's a good point. We've done so well so far that I hadn't really thought about what I'd do if we didn't solve a case." Hugh frowned. "I'm not sure I'd want to start working on the next case if we haven't solved this one."

"You can't think that way. We can only do our best with this case in the time we have to consider it. Whether we solve it or not, we'll have to move on next month."

"I wonder if Andrew will let us keep the file if we don't solve the case."

Thus far, Andrew had collected all of the case files from the unit members once the case was solved. He'd told Bessie that everything was taken back to London and shredded because it was highly confidential.

"I'm not sure he can." Bessie shook her head. "And I'm not going to worry about that for today. I'm going to remain optimistic that we're going to solve the case."

"I don't think anything we've done tonight is going to help with that."

"Except we've eliminated forty-eight people from consideration. We may have to go back through them and think again if we get stuck, but I'm fairly confident those forty-eight people were simply trying to have a nice time celebrating the season."

"That still leaves us with two people who need more investigating."

"Indeed. And maybe John and Doona found others in their pile of partygoers."

"Or maybe the killer was one of the staff. Maybe Harry and Charles found something interesting."

Bessie thought for a minute. "It still seems most likely that one of the three victims was the intended victim. I'm eager to read the statements from the people who were at the party with them."

"But that's a job for tomorrow," Hugh said, getting to his feet. He glanced at the clock and frowned. "No wonder I was falling asleep over the last few statements."

"It's been a long and very frustrating night. For the first time since the first case, I'm actually happy that I can't go and interview the witnesses myself. These witnesses, anyway. I'd love to talk to the friends and family members of the victims, but I'm quite happy I didn't have to talk to these fifty people."

"You don't even want to talk to Albert and Harold?"

Bessie chuckled. "Not really. While it's possible that Albert was the intended victim and that Harold was the killer, they both seemed to be quite unpleasant people."

"I'll see you at the unit meeting tomorrow, then," Hugh said as Bessie walked him to the door.

He gave her a hug, and then Bessie watched as he walked to his car. As he slowly drove away, she waved and then shut the door and locked it. After checking that the back door was also locked, Bessie turned the ringer off on the phone and headed for the stairs.

Turning off the ringer was her one concession to her age. After nearly falling down the stairs one night after she'd gone to bed early with a book, only to be interrupted by a loudly ringing telephone, she'd decided that she was better off not hearing it once she'd gone up to bed. The decision had been made easier by the fact that the call she'd raced to answer had been a man selling double glazing. She'd politely given him a stern lecture about ringing people late at night before turning off the ringer for the very first time.

Now she got ready for bed and crawled under the duvet. Her hand hovered over the book she was currently enjoying before she decided that she needed sleep more than she needed to read the next chapter. Switching off the light, she snuggled down and shut her eyes.

CHAPTER 6

When Bessie's eyes opened just a few minutes before six the next morning, the first thing she remembered was the conversation she needed to have with Eugene. She rolled over and squeezed her eyes shut, trying to put the unpleasant task out of her head. Then she sighed as she remembered the cold case that the unit was considering.

"A missing person and a seemingly unsolvable cold case. It's probably raining as well," she muttered to herself as she pushed back the duvet.

She got ready for the day without bothering to look outside. After patting on rose-scented dusting powder that reminded her of the man she'd loved and lost, Bessie headed down the stairs. When she reached the kitchen, she was surprised to see that the sun was coming up and that there were only a few scattered clouds in the sky.

"Maybe I should consider that a sign," she said as she poured herself some cereal. "Maybe I'll find Silvester today and we'll solve the cold case by the end of the fortnight."

While Bessie didn't really believe in signs, she was feeling slightly more optimistic as she got ready for her walk. The beach was empty, which wasn't surprising, considering the early hour. She walked as far as the stairs to Thie yn Traie and then decided to walk just a little bit farther. As she walked, she glanced up at the mansion above her.

It had originally been built as an extravagant summer home for a wealthy family from the UK. After one of the family members had been murdered on the island, they'd put the house on the market. It had sat empty for many months before Bessie's friends George and Mary Quayle had purchased the property. They also owned a huge house in Douglas, but as soon as they'd bought Thie yn Traie, they'd made the move to Laxey.

George was a loud, boisterous man who loved people and parties. His wife, Mary, was quiet and shy and preferred to stay at home, surrounded by her children and grandchildren. Bessie often wondered how the couple continued to make their marriage work in spite of their differences, but she knew that they were devoted to one another.

Nearly a year ago, after the murder of George's former business associate, the pair had taken an extended holiday. During that time, Mary had fallen ill, and they'd spent a large part of their time away seeking the best possible medical treatment for her. Now that they were back, Mary was slowly recovering, but she was still very susceptible to illness, so Bessie had barely seen her dear friend in the months since she'd returned to the island.

They'd managed to have a light lunch together, though, the day before Andrew had arrived for the latest cold case meeting. They'd also made plans to do the same again once Andrew had gone. Bessie could only hope that she'd be able to spend time with her friend regularly now that Mary was finally feeling better.

As she turned around to head for home, Bessie found

herself thinking about Mary's youngest child. Elizabeth was Mary's only daughter. Elizabeth had two older brothers, both of whom now worked with their father, helping to manage his many business concerns. When Bessie had first met Elizabeth, the young woman had just dropped out of her third university, and she was spending her time drinking in the local pubs with friends who visited regularly from across.

Bessie had been surprised, but supportive, when Elizabeth decided to start a party planning business on the island. Privately, Bessie had very much doubted that the island needed such a service, but she'd been happily proven wrong almost immediately as the business became a huge success very quickly. Part of that success came because Elizabeth was able to offer her clients some of the island's best catering. Andy Caine was a very talented young chef, and he and Elizabeth had developed both a personal and a professional relationship.

As Bessie walked back past the cottages, she shook her head to clear it. Now wasn't the time to be thinking about Andy and Elizabeth. She needed to focus on Silvester and Marion for the moment. That thought triggered a memory.

Bessie smiled to herself as she recalled a young Silvester splashing through the water, shouting at his sister as he went. Marion had been quite happy playing on the sand, but Silvester had been insistent that she had to join him in the sea. Bessie had been much younger in those days, and she'd had little experience with children. She could remember watching the pair and wondering who would win, but no matter how hard she tried, she couldn't recall what had happened next.

"Their mother probably took them both home," she muttered to herself as she reached the door to her cottage. "It can't possibly matter, anyway, whatever happened."

She filled the time until half ten by going back through

the last set of ten statements from the previous evening. Knowing she'd been tired when she'd read them, she went through them again to be certain that she hadn't missed anything.

"Nothing," she said when she was done. "Even wide awake, there isn't anything interesting in anything any of them said."

She looked at the clock. With a few minutes left to go, she filled the kettle and then made herself some tea. Then she settled in the chair next to the telephone and carefully dialled the number that Marion had given her.

"Hello?" The voice on the other end barked out the word.

Bessie frowned. She'd been expecting the other person to answer with the name of the restaurant. "Yes, hello," she said. "I'd like to speak to Eugene."

"This is Eugene. Is this Elizabeth Cubbon?"

"It is, yes."

"Very good. Marion told me that you'd be ringing. She said that you were an expert in finding missing people."

"Ah, well, um, Marion might have exaggerated slightly."

The man laughed. "I don't know Marion well, but I'm not surprised. I am grateful, though, that she's doing something about her brother's disappearance."

"You are?"

There was a short pause before the man spoke again. "I probably shouldn't have put it quite that way. The thing is, I didn't want to worry Marion."

"Worry her about what? She said when she rang you that you told her that Silvester had taken a few days off."

"Yes, that's right. He has," the man said slowly.

"But you're worried about him."

"I am a bit worried about him, yeah."

"Why?"

There was another pause before the man spoke again. "He's been seeing someone for a short while."

"And you don't care for the woman?" Bessie guessed.

"I wouldn't say that, not exactly."

"What would you say?" Bessie felt as if she was having to work far too hard to get the man to talk.

"She seems very nice, but I don't totally trust her," Eugene said eventually.

"Why don't you tell me about her?"

"I don't even know where to start."

Bessie swallowed a sigh. "Do you know her name?"

"Yeah, she's called Kalynn Swanson." He spelled both names for her. Bessie carefully wrote them down.

"And how old is she?"

"She's forty-something, or, at least, that's what she said when it came up in conversation. I suspect she may be closer to fifty-something, but I wasn't about to argue with her."

"Can you describe her?"

"She's blonde, but it isn't natural. She's about average height and weight. She wears a lot of makeup and too much perfume and she dresses as if she were still a teenager."

"How long has she been seeing Silvester?"

"I don't know. Not very long, but long enough for him to be stupid about her."

"Marion seemed to think that Silvester would have told her about any woman that he went out with more than a few times."

Eugene laughed. "If he'd done that, Silvester would have never stopped talking about the women in his life."

"Oh?"

"Silvester does really well with the ladies. I wish I knew why, because he's sort of average-looking and he spends most of his money on drinking, but he's never short of female company."

"Have any of his relationships been anything serious?"

"Nah, not with Silvester. He told me all about his marriages and his ex-wives. He didn't want to go through all of that again, so he kept things simple. He'd take a woman out a few times, but if she started getting serious, he'd end things right away."

"Charming," Bessie said flatly.

"Yeah, well, it was better than marrying them and then divorcing them. Silvester enjoyed falling in love, but he never managed to stay in love for long."

"And he's been involved with a lot of different women since he's been in Liverpool?"

"He has, indeed. I used to tease him that he was going to have to move away because he was going to run out of women here."

"And then he met Kalynn."

Eugene sighed. "Yeah, and then he met Kalynn."

"Do you know how they met?"

"She came in to get dinner with some friends one night. I can't remember what she ordered, but whatever it was, she enjoyed it so much that she asked her waiter if she could thank the chef personally. Silvester went out to talk to her and by the time he went back into the kitchen, he was hooked."

"How long ago was that?"

"Probably about a fortnight ago. I can try to pin it down more exactly if you really need it."

"I might, but we can get back to that later. What can you tell me about the friends she was with that evening?"

"Not one thing. She'd made the booking in her name, and she paid the bill with her credit card. I only remember that because Silvester mentioned it later. He said something about her being such a kind and generous friend that she'd bought dinner for six in our restaurant. He said they were there to celebrate someone's new job, but that's all I know."

"And the friends haven't been back to the restaurant since?"

"I suppose they might have been. I probably wouldn't recognise any of them if they did come in. None of them made any impression on me the night they were there. Kalynn didn't really, either, aside from asking to thank the chef."

"Does that happen often?"

"It happens a few times every year. It was out of the ordinary, but not completely unheard of. I'm the manager of the restaurant, and the waiter didn't bother to tell me about the request. He simply told Silvester and our head chef, and they agreed that Silvester would go and talk to Kalynn."

"Was that unusual? Who normally talks to customers who want to see the chef?"

"That depends on the customer. We have some guests who dine with us regularly. If they ask to see the chef, the head chef goes out to speak to them. Other guests, especially ones who are not known to us, are usually met by an assistant chef. I'm sure you can understand how busy our head chef is during the dinner service. He simply doesn't have time to meet with guests unless it is absolutely necessary."

"So they met and Silvester was immediately attracted to Kalynn. What happened next?"

"He asked her to have lunch with him the next day. They did that, and then had dinner the following day when Silvester had a night off from work. After that, Kalynn had to go away for a few days. It was something to do with work, or so she told Silvester, anyway."

"You don't sound as if you believed her."

"I didn't really give it much thought at the time, but now

that Silvester is missing, I'm questioning everything I know about Kalynn."

"What does she do for work?"

"According to Silvester, she works with computers for some big company, but he couldn't tell me which one."

"That's odd."

"He told me that Kalynn had told him, but he'd forgotten. I suppose that's possible, because he always drank a lot when he was with Kalynn."

"Did he? That makes it sound as if he wasn't enjoying her company."

"I think it was more because she encouraged him to drink a lot when they were together. Silvester said that she'd told him that she thought he was more fun when he was a little bit drunk."

"How dreadful."

"I thought so, too, but Silvester seemed to find it funny."

"Do you know where she lives?"

"Silvester said that she had a flat nearby, but he never told me more than that. From what he said, I don't think he'd ever been to her flat. I know she'd been to his because she made a comment one night in the bar about how untidy it had been."

"When was that?"

"Last week. Silvester met up with her as soon as she'd landed in Liverpool. She came into the bar the next night, towards the end of his shift. She had a few drinks while she waited for him."

"And you had a conversation with her?"

"A very short one. I asked her how her trip had been, and she said it had been okay. Then I asked where she'd gone, and she said Birmingham. When I asked where in Birmingham, she just shook her head and then changed the subject."

"To what?"

"She asked me about my socks, actually. I have a collection of fun socks, and I wear them at work. Normally, no one sees them because my trouser legs cover them, but everyone who works at the restaurant knows about them."

"And Silvester told Kalynn about them."

"I assume so. Anyway, she asked what I was wearing, and then we had a short chat about the characters on the socks. Then she mentioned that she'd seen similar socks in Silvester's flat. She said something like 'His flat is such a mess. There were socks everywhere.'"

"So she's been to his flat."

"Yeah, and then Silvester finished working and they went out of the restaurant arm in arm."

"What happened next?"

"The next day, Silvester came in and asked for a few days off this week. He hadn't taken any holiday time for a while, and we're pretty quiet this time of year, so I said he could have the time off. He didn't mention Kalynn. I'm sorry now that I didn't ask what he was planning to do on his holiday."

"Did you see Kalynn again after that?"

"No, I haven't seen her since, and I got the impression that Silvester hadn't seen her either."

"Oh?"

"He just made a stray comment about spending his nights alone, that's all. I should have asked him about Kalynn, but I was hoping that they'd ended things, and I didn't want to pry."

"So why don't you like her?"

"Like I said, I just don't trust her. There is something shifty about her."

"Do you think she's kidnapped Silvester for some reason?"

There was a long silence on the other end of the phone. Eventually, Eugene spoke again. "That never even crossed my mind. I sort of just assumed that they'd gone somewhere together and were drinking too much and ignoring their mobiles. Having said that, maybe Kalynn is answering hers. Silvester seems to be ignoring his, though."

"And that idea worries you?"

Eugene sighed. "Silvester has a drinking problem. He manages it reasonably well. He never drinks when he has to work the next day, for example, but when he does get a few days off in a row, he has been known to behave badly."

"How badly?"

"He's been banned from some of the pubs in the area for fighting," Eugene explained. "But he's always paid restitution for anything he's broken."

"And now you're worried that he's somewhere with Kalynn, drinking too much."

"Exactly. Silvester is a good person and a great chef as long as he stays sober. That Kalynn encourages him to drink is probably the thing that bothers me the most about her."

"That is quite worrying."

"What are you going to do next?"

Bessie frowned. "I'm not sure. Marion doesn't want to file a missing person report."

"He did ask for the time off. He may show up for work on Friday as expected and laugh when I tell him that we were worried about him."

"I may have a friend of mine make a few discreet enquires between now and Friday. Please ring me when he does return to work." She gave him her number. "I really hope that Marion is worrying over nothing, but what you've told me is also somewhat concerning."

"If I can do anything else to help, please let me know," Eugene told her.

Bessie put the phone down and then frowned at it. "Everything is probably fine," she said loudly before she picked the receiver back up and dialled Marion's number.

She repeated the words to Marion. "Everything is probably fine, but I'm going to talk to a friend of mine, just in case."

"What friend?"

"Andrew is a former Scotland Yard inspector."

"The head of the cold case unit? You're going to talk to him about my missing brother?"

"I'm going to ask him to make a few discreet enquires about your brother and the woman with whom he may be spending his time."

"What did Eugene tell you?"

Bessie thought for a minute. "He said that Silvester had met a woman recently, but that they'd only gone out a few times. He had her name, so I'm going to ask Andrew to see if he can find her."

"Eugene thinks something terrible has happened to Silvester, doesn't he?"

"Not at all. He thinks Silvester is with his new friend."

Marion sighed. "I'm trying not to worry, but it's hard. Silvester is the most wonderful person in the world so long as he isn't drinking."

"So hopefully, wherever he is, he isn't drinking."

Marion snorted. "If he's not working, he's drinking," she said. "And he isn't working."

"If you hear from him, let me know," Bessie told her.

"I will. He won't ring me when he's been drinking, though. He knows I don't approve. That's why I always want him to come home when he takes time off work. He knows better than to show up at my house drunk, and, back when he lived here, he was banned from every pub in the north of the island, so he can't go out and get drunk once he gets here, either."

"He doesn't drink at home?"

"Not in my home, and he always stays with me when he comes across."

"I'll ring you if I learn anything. Eugene said he was due back at work on Friday. If he doesn't turn up for work, I think you should definitely file a missing person report."

"Yeah, that's a good idea. Even when he's at his most irresponsible, Silvester takes his work seriously."

But what if someone else is encouraging him to be irresponsible? Bessie wondered as she put down the phone.

A knock on the door had her on her feet a minute later.

"Andrew, hello," she said.

"I was wondering if you wanted to join me for lunch before the unit meeting," he said. "Helen and I were going to go somewhere, but something has gone badly wrong at work so she can't get away."

"I'd like that, but I'll warn you that I have something I want to discuss with you over lunch."

"That sounds ominous."

"I hope it isn't anything too bad, but it is something worrying."

"To do with the cold case or the unit?"

"Oh, no. I just have a friend with a missing brother."

Andrew frowned. "Maybe we should ask Charles to join us."

"That's up to you. I need a few minutes to get ready."

"I'll meet you at my car in fifteen minutes."

Bessie nodded and then shut the door. In her bedroom, she changed into an outfit she deemed appropriate for the unit meeting and then combed her hair and refreshed her lipstick. Then she grabbed her case file and headed back down the stairs. She was standing next to Andrew's hire car when he emerged from his holiday cottage.

CHAPTER 7

"Charles is having lunch with Harry," Andrew told her as they climbed into the car. "They're going back over a few things they found in their section of the statements."

"I wish Hugh and I had found anything that needed a second look," Bessie replied. She fastened her seatbelt and then waited for Andrew to start the car.

"I fancy fish and chips. Where is the best place to get fish and chips between here and Ramsey?"

"There is an excellent chippy in Ramsey. Just drive as if you were going to the Seaview, and I'll tell you where to turn."

A short while later the pair were sitting on the Ramsey promenade with their lunch.

"Tell me about your missing person, then," Andrew invited.

Bessie quickly took him through everything that she'd learned so far. When she was done, she sighed. "I'm not sure what to do next. The man might not even be missing. He might turn up for work on Friday and be amazed that anyone was worried about him."

"I think you're right to be concerned, though. That he missed Marion's birthday is worrying, and you said that Eugene is concerned as well. I'll ring a few people I know in Liverpool and see if anyone knows anything about Kalynn Swanson."

"I'd appreciate that."

The pair ate in companionable silence for a few minutes.

"From what you said earlier, I take it you didn't find anything interesting in your witness statements last night," Andrew said after he'd finished the last of his fish.

Bessie shook her head. "We found one person we thought might have been the intended victim. He was at the party with his business partner, and both of them admitted that they'd been arguing recently. That seems a long way from bringing poison to a party and deliberately killing innocent people while attempting to kill your partner, though."

Andrew nodded. "It takes a special kind of evil to do something like what was done at the party. Murder is always dreadful, but killing strangers just to hide your intention is particularly horrible."

"It has allowed the killer to get away with it for five years. I just hope we'll be able to work out what happened and finally put him or her behind bars."

"I'm looking forward to hearing from all three of the teams today. If John and Doona only found one or two other possible victims, then we've already eliminated a great many suspects."

"Surely we should be focused on the men and women who were at the party with the victims."

"And they will be our main focus now that we've had a preliminary look at everyone else. One of Theodore's main concerns was that he missed something because he did put most of his attention on the people who'd been at the party with the victims. It was important that we consider the others first and identify any that might be of interest."

Bessie nodded. "Hugh and I were curious what the bartender who served the poisoned drinks had to say."

"You'll get his statement today. I didn't even share that one with Harry and Charles, even though they got all of the other members of staff."

"I didn't realise that."

"There isn't anything helpful in it, but you already knew that because we're considering the case."

Bessie sighed. "I suppose I was rather hoping that he'd seen something that might narrow down the list of suspects, but if he had, we would have started there, wouldn't we?"

"Probably. As it is, I thought it made sense for us to start with the entire pool of suspects and work from there."

"We eliminated a lot because not that many people were drinking dry white wine."

Andrew nodded. "Theodore did the same thing, but, when we last talked, he asked me if he thought he'd been wise to do so."

"And what did you say?"

"That I'd probably have done the same thing under the circumstances. There are all sorts of possibilities, of course, but we have to work with the ones that seem the most likely."

Bessie ate the last of her chips and then wiped her fingers. "That was delicious."

"It was very good, but now I feel as if I need a long walk to make up for eating it."

"We should have time to walk to the end of the promenade and back, anyway."

They strolled slowly, stopping for ice cream before they reached the end of the broad walkway.

"And now I have to make up for this, too," Andrew said with a laugh as they walked away from the ice cream stand.

"But it's so good," Bessie said. "We just have to hope that Jasper has given us only biscuits today."

"Plain digestives, ideally stale ones."

Bessie laughed. "I don't think Jasper would do that."

"We'll have to see when we get there," Andrew said as they reached his car.

They made the short drive to the Seaview, arriving a few minutes early. Inside the hotel, Jasper was behind the reception desk again.

"Ah, good afternoon," he said.

"And how are you today?" Bessie asked.

He laughed. "Remember what I said about the chef and the pastry chef? Last night they decided that their temporary truce was over. Chef very nearly quit, and the pastry chef did quit. I was very tempted to let them both go, too, but Stuart wouldn't hear of it."

"I am sorry," Bessie said.

Jasper shrugged. "While I hate having to spend all of my time trying to get those two to get along, I also hated sitting around waiting for the inevitable fight."

"But now you don't have a pastry chef," Bessie said.

"I'm working on getting him back, of course, but, in the meantime, the head chef decided to prove to me that we don't need him by baking for you for today."

"Oh? I knew we shouldn't have had that ice cream," Bessie said.

"Don't be too sure about that. Chef hasn't done puddings in a while. Let's just say he was a bit out of practice and leave it at that."

"What does that mean?" Bessie demanded.

Jasper grinned. "If I tell you that we had the fire department here earlier because someone left a tray of biscuits in the oven for far too long, you'll know why I don't want to talk about it."

"Oh, my," Bessie said.

"You're in the penthouse conference room again," Jasper told them. "If I can't give you amazing food, at least I can give you amazing views."

"I'm sure whatever we've been given will be lovely," Bessie said as she and Andrew turned towards the lifts.

"I hope the meeting goes well," was Jasper's reply.

When they reached the conference room, they found Hugh already at the table. He had a plate with a handful of biscuits and cakes on it at his elbow.

"Good afternoon," Bessie said. "What should we try first?" she asked, gesturing towards the table at the back of the room.

Hugh made a face. "Whatever looks good?" he replied, making the statement sound as if it were a question.

"Is something not good?" Bessie asked.

Hugh shrugged. "It's all okay, but none of it is up to the Seaview's usual standards. I'll eat what I've taken, but I don't plan to go back for more."

Bessie didn't bother to hide her surprise. "It must be quite dreadful, then," she exclaimed.

"It's not dreadful," Hugh assured her. "It just isn't moreish."

Andrew selected a few of the treats and then poured himself a cup of coffee. Bessie cautiously picked out some of the things that looked the best and then got herself some tea. As they sat down at the table, John and Doona walked in. Hugh told them about the food while they got themselves drinks.

"Is it really that bad?" Doona asked Bessie, who'd just taken a bite of biscuit.

Bessie frowned. "It isn't bad, exactly, but it isn't very good."

They were talking about the treats when Harry and Charles joined them a few minutes later. The new arrivals got drinks and then joined the others at the table.

"Tell me that one of you found something interesting, please," Charles said after a sip of his coffee.

Bessie shook her head. "We found one man that we thought might have been the intended victim, in that he and his business partner were at the party together and had been fighting, but otherwise the statements were full of people who didn't see anything, didn't know any of the victims, and couldn't help the police in any way."

Doona nodded. "We had much the same thing. We had one couple who were teetering on the brink of divorce. The husband was drinking dry white wine, which was apparently very annoying to the wife for some inexplicable reason, but they both swore that neither of them had gone anywhere near the bar at the back of the room or the food table."

"But they couldn't prove it, could they?" Hugh asked.

"No, but apparently the food was one of the things they were fighting about," Doona told him. "The wife thought the invitation included a sit-down dinner, and she was upset that all they were offered was a buffet. She told the police that she refused to eat buffet food because you never know who'd sneezed on everything just before you got there."

Bessie made a face. "What about the husband? Surely, if they were fighting, he should have gone and filled a plate."

John grinned. "He was planning on it, but he was too busy fighting with her about his choice of drink, and about her shoes, and about what she'd bought for his mother for Christmas, to actually get to the food before the first victim fell."

"Do we have updates on everyone?" Bessie asked Andrew. "I really want to know what happened to those two."

"We do have updates on everyone. I'll give you copies of all of the updates, but I suggest you focus on the people whom we've flagged as possibly being of interest."

Bessie nodded. "One of these days, after we've solved the case, I want to read through all of the other statements and all of the updates. I'm really curious if being a witness to murders changed anyone's life."

"First we have to solve the case," Harry said. "Charles and I spent a long time going through the statements from the hotel staff. None of them were willing to admit to having seen anything out of the ordinary, but we were expecting that. What we were hoping to find was a hint that one of them was behind the killings."

"Did any of them know any of the victims?" Doona asked.

"None of them admitted to knowing any of the victims," Harry told her. "But remember that everyone who was invited to the party had been a guest at the hotel during the year. As guests, they would have encountered many different members of staff during their stay."

"All of the guests were asked if they remembered any particular members of staff from their visit or from the party," Doona said. "None of them could remember any member of staff by name, although a few said things like 'The woman at reception was very nice,' or 'We had a waiter who was helpful.'"

Bessie nodded. "We had similar remarks in our statements, but, again, none of the guests admitted to remembering any particular member of staff."

"Which is not to say that one or more of them didn't make an impression on a member of staff," Harry said. "These were mostly wealthy people who were accustomed to having staff around to see to their needs. Maybe one of the

THE LAWRENCE FILE

members of staff found one or more of them too demanding."

"So did anyone on the staff team raise your suspicions?" Andrew asked.

Harry and Charles exchanged glances. "We have a short list of three members of staff about whom we'd like more information," Harry said. "They're probably totally innocent, but there were small things in their statements that caught our attention."

Andrew nodded. "I'll take the list back to Theodore. He can have someone take a closer look at the three of them as we continue working through the case file."

Harry handed Andrew a slip of paper.

"Hugh and Bessie identified one man as the possible intended victim," Andrew said. "And John and Doona have done the same. Why don't you tell us about the people you found?"

John looked at Doona and then shrugged. "The couple are Bill and Dorothy Hughes. Bill was forty-eight and Dorothy was forty-three on the night of the party. They'd been married for six years, and it was a second marriage for both of them."

"And Bill was a horrible person," Doona added. "He probably still is, but he definitely was five years ago."

"To be fair to Bill, Dorothy was quite dreadful, too," John said.

Doona sighed. "Yes, you're right, but she was probably perfectly lovely before she married Bill."

John chuckled. "If she truly did marry Bill for his money, as Bill suggested, then I doubt she was perfectly lovely before they married."

"But he was a terrible snob who never thought anything she did was good enough," Doona said. "And, according to

Dorothy, her first husband had more money than Bill, anyway."

"Too bad he didn't leave it to Dorothy when he died," John said.

Doona frowned. "Yes, okay, it is entirely possible that Dorothy only married Bill for his money. Actually, now that I think about it, it seems likely that she only married him for his money. Why else would she want to marry such a deeply unpleasant person?"

"A better question might be why he married her," Charles suggested.

Doona shrugged. "The investigator who took their statements didn't ask them that."

"Didn't you say earlier that he was the one drinking dry white wine?" Harry asked.

Doona nodded.

"So if he was the intended victim, she murdered three innocent people," Harry said.

"Okay, so maybe she wasn't a nice person, but I still think at least some of that came from being married to a nasty man," Doona said.

"Is it possible that someone else at the party wanted to kill Bill Hughes?" Harry asked.

"Anyone who knew him?" Doona suggested.

Everyone laughed.

"Did either of them know anyone else at the party?" Harry asked.

"Not according to their statements," John said. "Dorothy mentioned having met one or two of the other guests before, but she said she didn't actually know any of them. Bill said he'd probably met some of the others before, but he didn't remember any of them and hadn't had any intention of speaking to any of them at the party."

"Why were they at the party, then?" Bessie asked.

"They had come to London to do some shopping. They lived in Scotland, but visited London several times a year. They'd already been planning a December trip when they received the invitation to the Christmas party. According to Bill, they decided they might as well go to the party since they were already going to be there."

"And, according to Dorothy, they both thought the party included a sit-down dinner with multiple courses. They claimed that they'd attended in previous years and that the party had always had a sit-down meal."

"Not to interrupt, but Theodore did ask the hotel management about that. They'd been having the Christmas party for their most frequent guests for over thirty years, and it had always included a buffet meal," Andrew added.

"How likely do you think it is that Bill was the intended victim?" Harry asked Doona and John.

John shook his head. "Unless there was someone else in the crowd who wanted Bill dead, I don't think he was the target. He and Dorothy weren't getting along, but, from what they both said, they hadn't been getting along for years. I can't see her choosing that evening to kill the man."

"And if she had, I can't see her killing innocent people along the way," Doona added.

John nodded. "She sounded as if she was shocked and horrified by what had happened. Of course, it's impossible to tell from reading her interview from years ago if her reaction was genuine, but I'd put her near the bottom of my list. I don't actually have a list yet, though."

Andrew nodded. "Bessie, tell us about Albert and Harold."

Bessie did her best to summarise what she and Hugh had read in their statements. "It seemed as if they were both angry with one another, but I don't think Harold was angry enough to kill Albert, let alone a few random strangers," she said in the end.

"Is that all that we got out of the initial read-through of the witness statements?" Andrew asked.

"I wish we'd found more," Hugh said. "But I'm also glad we didn't. I really think we're going to find the killer in the list of men and women who were with the victims."

"Except that's where Theodore has focused his attention for the past five years," Andrew said. "If the killer is there, I would have expected Theodore to have found him or her by now."

"Maybe he's just not asked the right questions," Hugh said.

"Maybe. Does anyone have anything they want to add before we talk briefly about the victims and their companions?" Andrew asked.

"I'd like a chance to read through the rest of the statements," Harry said. "I know there are a hundred of them, but I want to see every bit of information that's available about this case."

Bessie nodded. "I feel the same way, even though just doing fifty of them was exhausting."

Andrew grinned. "I suspected that you'd all feel that way, so I've printed copies of everything for everyone. I'll give you those today, along with the statements from the victims' friends and family and from the man who was tending bar where the poisoned bottle was discovered. We aren't meeting tomorrow, so that should give you time to work through at least some of the extra statements after you've read the ones from the victims' companions."

"Excellent," Harry said.

CHAPTER 8

"Before I give you the statements, I want to give you a quick introduction to the men and women involved," Andrew said. "Let's start with the bartender, Joseph Sable."

"A few of the other members of staff mentioned him," Charles said. "He wasn't well liked, but everyone agreed that he did his job well. I got the impression that he wasn't very friendly, though."

Andrew nodded. "Joseph was forty-six on the night of the Christmas party. He'd been working as a bartender since he'd left school with only a few qualifications. He'd started in a local pub, where he spent as much time breaking up fights as he did serving drinks. Over the years, he'd gradually moved to nicer and nicer establishments. Unlike some of the people working at the party, he was employed by the hotel. He usually worked behind the hotel's main bar, serving drinks five nights a week."

"Some of the people working that night were from an agency?" John asked.

"Yes, although only a few," Andrew replied. "It was a large

luxury hotel, so they had a considerable number of staff on their books. For the party, they had just about every employee working, including many who typically worked only part-time for them. Only a handful of the serving staff were from an agency, and they were primarily tasked with clearing away the empty plates and glasses that people were leaving everywhere."

Charles chuckled. "And they were very vocal about just how inconsiderate the guests were," he said. "One woman went on a lengthy rant about guests putting empty glasses on the floor behind a row of Christmas trees. She seemed to think that some of the guests were going out of their way to be difficult."

"Why would you put an empty glass on the floor behind a Christmas tree?" Bessie asked.

Charles shrugged.

Bessie shook her head. "But you were telling us about Joseph Sable," she reminded Andrew.

"Yes, where was I? He comes across in his interview as rather jaded about life, but also somewhat shaken by what had happened. I'll leave you to read the statement and draw your own conclusions," he replied.

"Theodore must have taken a really hard look at him," Harry said.

Andrew nodded. "Of course, he could easily have added the poison to the bottle, which made him the most obvious suspect. Theodore spent a lot of time and resources trying to find a link between him and any one of the victims, though, and failed."

"Maybe he just wanted to see what it felt like to kill someone," Harry said.

"Sadly, that is a possibility, but there is nothing in his background to suggest that he's unstable," Andrew said.

"If it was that random, we'll never find the killer," Charles said.

Harry shook his head. "If Theodore keeps pushing and asking questions, sooner or later he might get a break."

"Is there anything else you want to tell us about Joseph?" Bessie asked, looking up from her notes.

Andrew shook his head. "You can read his statement for yourselves. We'll talk about him again on Friday."

"So that just leaves the victims and their friends and family members," Doona said.

Bessie flipped back a few pages in her notebook. "You already told us a little bit about them," she said.

"And maybe that's enough for now," Andrew said. "On Friday, I'll share updates on where all of the friends and family members are now."

"I'd like to see where everyone was standing in relation to the bar," Harry said. "I've been trying to visualise it all, but I can't."

"I can ask Jasper if we can use the ballroom for another reconstruction," Andrew said. "That's actually a really good idea. The ballroom here is larger than the room where they had the party. I think it would help clarify a lot if we could see how the room was laid out and where everyone was standing when people started dying."

"We'll do that on Friday?" Harry asked.

Andrew nodded. "We'll do that on Friday, either before or after we talk about the main suspects."

"Is that all for today, then?" Charles asked as he began to pack up his things.

"I suppose so, unless anyone has any questions," Andrew replied.

"I think we're all eager to get properly started on the case," Harry said as Andrew began to pass out envelopes.

"Even though we've been working on it for twenty-four hours, it doesn't feel as if we've done anything useful yet."

Andrew nodded. "I hope these statements will be more interesting for you."

"They can't be more boring," Hugh said under his breath as he took his envelope from Andrew.

Harry and Charles were the first to leave the room. John and Doona weren't far behind. They stopped to give Bessie hugs before they left. Hugh got up, and then frowned and sat back down.

"What's wrong?" Bessie asked.

"I always take things home from our meetings, cakes or biscuits or pie – or remember those wonderful little balls of pudding that the pastry chef did that one time? I love taking things home from the Seaview," he said.

"But you didn't like any of the things we were given today," Bessie suggested.

Hugh shook his head. "Not really. Some of it was okay, but none of it was wonderful. I like surprising Grace with wonderful things, especially now that she's working so hard to make another baby."

"So stop at a bakery on your way home," Bessie suggested.

"Yeah, that's a better idea than taking any of that home," Hugh said. As he walked out of the room, Jasper walked in.

"Knock, knock," he said. "I hope I'm not interrupting."

"Not at all," Bessie replied. "We're just packing up slowly."

Jasper did a quick survey of the table at the back of the room. "Was it that bad?" he asked. "This looks barely touched."

"I only tried a few things, and they were fine," Bessie told him. "Fine, but not wonderful. I didn't bother going back for more."

Jasper sighed. "We can't serve any of this to our guests, then. I know Chef can make good puddings when he tries, but he isn't in the mood to try. I need to get the pastry chef back, but he's ignoring his phone."

"Maybe you should go and visit him," Bessie suggested.

Jasper grinned. "Or I could send Stuart. It isn't as if he's doing anything. He can go and talk to the pastry chef. This is all his fault, anyway."

Bessie started to question the comment and then shut her mouth. It wasn't any of her business and she didn't want to pry, not when she had case files to read, anyway.

Jasper walked with them to the lifts and then back through the hotel to the lobby.

"Thank you for letting us use the penthouse again," Bessie told him at the door.

"Is there any chance we can use the ballroom on Friday?" Andrew asked.

"The ballroom? Are you planning a party?" Jasper replied.

"We want to try re-creating a party, actually," Andrew told him. "We have pictures and floor plans, but we're all struggling to picture the room and the layout."

"I know we don't have any events on Friday afternoon in the ballroom, but it's possible that someone has booked a wedding consultation that would include a tour of the ballroom. Give me a minute to check," Jasper said.

"If we can't use the ballroom here, are there other hotels on the island with similarly large spaces?" Andrew asked Bessie.

"Most of the hotels on the island that used to have ballrooms have converted them into spas or restaurants or bars. Very few people hold events that need spaces as large at the ballroom here."

"So we may have to get creative."

"I think the great room at Thie yn Traie might be large enough," Bessie said thoughtfully. "And if it isn't, I suspect there might be a room in the Quayles' Douglas mansion that would fit the bill."

Andrew nodded. "What about the house that we visited with your friend Andy Caine? There was a large foyer, but probably not large enough."

Bessie thought for a minute. "Andy is buying the house," she told him. "But the sale hasn't gone through yet. I'm sure Hilary would let us use the space, though, if we needed to. Having said that, I don't think any of the rooms were large enough."

"I'm glad to hear that Andy is buying the house. It seemed perfect for what he wants to do."

"It's a bit of a drive from Douglas, but, otherwise, it's wonderful."

"And Andy has been looking for the perfect location for a long time, hasn't he?"

Bessie nodded. Once Andy had finished culinary school, he'd come back to the island with big plans to buy both a house and a restaurant. Instead, he'd begun catering for Elizabeth Quayle, enjoying both a personal and professional relationship with her. They'd ended both when Elizabeth had decided to join her parents on their extended holiday. As soon as Elizabeth had gone, someone else had set her sights on Andy, though.

The woman had been calling herself Jennifer Johnson, and she'd started her own party planning business and talked Andy into catering for her almost immediately. Then she'd done her best to charm him while filling his head with lies about Elizabeth. Andy had been naïve enough to believe Jennifer's lies and before the truth finally came out, he'd asked Jennifer to marry him. Once Andy learned the truth, Jennifer had fled the island, and Andy had left soon after to do some travelling and clear his head.

On his return to the island, he'd started over, looking for

a house for himself and a location for his future business. Bessie had been delighted when he'd found an almost perfect building that would work as both. The house was in Lonan, and it belonged to a woman that Bessie knew. Hilary was eager for a quick sale, and Bessie was sure the property would be a good investment for Andy.

"He was afraid of making the wrong decision," Bessie explained to Andrew.

"In that case, I'm surprised he's actually agreed to buy anything."

Bessie laughed. "He only agreed because he asked Elizabeth for her opinion."

"Ah, are they back together, then?"

"Not at all, but he wanted to know what she thought of the property anyway. He has a lot of respect for her business sense."

"And she told him to buy it?"

"She was much smarter than that. She told him that if he didn't snap it up, she was going to buy it."

Andrew laughed. "That's very clever, actually. So Andy is buying Hilary's house. What about Elizabeth? Is she buying anything?"

"She and George have been talking about turning the house in Douglas into an event centre. I don't know if they've actually done anything about it yet, but the last time I talked to Elizabeth, that was the plan."

"That seems a good idea, too."

Bessie nodded, and then smiled at Jasper as he walked towards them.

"I'm sorry to have kept you waiting," he said when he reached them. "There was something illegible on the calendar, which meant I had to ring a few people to try to find out what it was."

"And what was it?" Bessie asked.

Jasper grinned. "A desperate doodle by an overworked front desk employee," he said with a laugh. "It isn't as bad as it sounds. One of the young men who works at the front desk ended up talking for far too long to an older woman who simply wanted to chat more than anything else. Oh, she booked a room for a night, too, but the conversation took nearly an hour. Mark knows all about the woman's children, who never ring her. About her grandchildren, who are just as bad. And about her nieces and nephews and cousins and more distant relatives. Also, her friends and neighbours and the woman who works in the local charity shop who always sits and has tea and biscuits with our future guest whenever she pops in."

Bessie laughed. "My goodness, poor Mark."

Jasper nodded. "He was delighted to hear that all of the people I just mentioned are going to be very disappointed when our guest passes away. According to what she told Mark, she's leaving everything she has to the woman who works at the charity shop."

"Good for her," Bessie said.

Andrew nodded. "I sometimes complain about how often my children and grandchildren ring me, but I'm grateful that they still want to speak to me and sometimes even value my opinion. I'm sure your future guest is simply lonely."

"Yes, I shall make a point of chatting with her when she arrives. I love nothing more than hearing about other people's ungrateful children," Jasper said. "I shall have to invite Stuart to join us. He'll enjoy it, too."

"Does that mean that we can use the ballroom tomorrow?" Bessie asked.

Jasper nodded. "I've booked it in the system, which is new and barely being used, but I'm trying. I've also written it on the calendar, which is what we used to do before we bought the new computer system. What do you need besides space?"

Andrew thought for a minute. "We're going to need some tape that we can put down on the floor to mark out the dimensions of the room. It was a large rectangle, and there were bars along three of the four walls."

"If you have a floor plan, I can have the room set up for you before you arrive," Jasper offered.

"I don't want to give you extra work," Andrew replied.

Jasper shook his head. "The hotel is already significantly less busy than it was just a few weeks ago. I haven't cut back on restaurant staffing levels yet, though. Maybe I'll tell the chef and the pastry chef to do it, actually. It would be good for them to have to work together on something."

Andrew opened his briefcase and then opened a folder. After flipping through it, he found what he was looking for. He pulled a sheet of paper out and then studied it for a moment. "Is there somewhere where I could make you a copy of this?" he asked Jasper.

"I can make a copy," Jasper said, holding out a hand.

Andrew shook his head. "There are things I'm going to have to cover on the original before I make the copy."

Jasper grinned. "Oh, I forgot, this is all top secret. I can take you into the office. You can make your copy there. You can use sticky notes to cover up the things I can't see."

Andrew nodded, and then he and Jasper walked away, leaving Bessie on her own in the lobby. She sat down on one of the comfortable couches and settled back to enjoy the scenery. A moment later, the doors slid open, and a man walked into the room. Bessie frowned as he noticed her and walked closer.

"Bessie, here for a cold case meeting?" Dan Ross asked.

"No comment," Bessie told him.

Dan laughed. "I'm just making polite conversation. I couldn't care less why you're here. I have much more important stories to cover than your cold case unit."

Bessie raised an eyebrow. "Stories that involve the Seaview?"

"Wouldn't you like to know?"

"Actually, I don't much care. How are you, though?" While she didn't much care for the island's only investigative reporter, she couldn't help but be polite.

Dan looked slightly surprised by the question. "I'm fine," he replied after a moment. "Why? Did someone suggest otherwise?"

Bessie frowned. "No, not at all. Why? Have you been unwell?"

"No, not at all," Dan snapped. "I just thought people might be speculating about me since I'm single again."

"Ah." Bessie hadn't realised that he and his girlfriend had broken up, but she wasn't terribly surprised by the news. "I am sorry," she said.

"I'm not. Susie was a sweet girl, but she took up a lot of my time, and having a girlfriend was expensive, too. I'm better off on my own."

"She seemed very nice when I met her."

"But she didn't really like the island," Dan said sullenly. "And she didn't believe me when I said that I was going to be getting a job with one of the big papers across any day now."

Dan had been making that claim for years. As far as Bessie knew, his chances of getting a job across were slim to none. "Has Susie gone back across, then?"

"Yeah. Like I said, she didn't like the island. She missed her family, too."

"Life on a small island can be a big adjustment for some people."

Dan shrugged. "I suppose so. I did think she might agree to wait for me, but she said she couldn't live with the uncertainty of not knowing when I'd be moving. The story I'm working on now, though, is going to be the one. I just know it."

"I hope you're right," Bessie said sincerely. She would have been happy for both Dan and everyone else on the island if he ever did move across.

"Yeah, well, I'd better get back to work, then." Dan took a few steps away from Bessie and then looked back at her. "If anyone asks, you never saw me," he said, his eyes darting back and forth before he slunk away down the corridor that led to the restaurant at the back of the building.

Bessie was still trying to work out what Dan was investigating when Andrew rejoined her a minute later.

"Are we all set?" she asked as she stood up.

Andrew nodded. "Jasper is going to get the room ready for us before we get here tomorrow. I'm looking forward to seeing it, if you know what I mean."

"I know exactly what you mean. I've looked at the pictures dozens of times, but I still can't really imagine how anyone put the poison in the wine bottle."

"Hopefully, all will be revealed tomorrow."

They walked out of the hotel and back to Andrew's car. The drive to Laxey didn't take long.

"What now?" Andrew asked as he parked outside of Bessie's cottage.

"Now I get to read the statements that really matter," Bessie said. "I know that Theodore has been concentrating on these people, but I can't help but feel as if he must have missed something. The killer has to have been one of the people in this envelope." She held up her envelope and then opened her door.

Andrew grinned at her. "I'm going to go and read through the statements again myself, but I'm going to take a break for dinner. Would you care to join me?"

Bessie hesitated. "I suppose that will depend on how far I can get through the statements."

"You have to eat, regardless."

"Yes, I know. Okay, I'll join you for dinner."

"Why don't we go to the little Italian place here in Laxey? It's close to home and it's usually fairly quick."

"That sounds perfect. Will Helen be joining us?"

"Probably, but even if she doesn't, the restaurant is too small for us to be able to talk about the case over dinner."

Bessie nodded. "What time?"

"Half six?"

"I'll be ready."

She got out of the car and let herself into her cottage. After taking off her shoes, she filled the kettle and then made herself some tea.

"No biscuits. You're going for dinner soon," she told herself as the kettle boiled.

After carrying the tea into the sitting room and putting it next to her favourite chair, she went back into the kitchen and grabbed her envelope, her notebook, and a pen.

"And now, let's see what you all have to say for yourselves," she muttered as she opened the envelope.

CHAPTER 9

When someone knocked on her door, Bessie looked up and momentarily felt disorientated. She got to her feet and walked into the kitchen. A quick glance at the clock told her who was going to be at the door.

"I'm not ready," she told Andrew and Helen. "I was reading statements and I lost all track of time."

"We can wait while you get ready," Helen assured her.

Bessie nodded and then walked back into the sitting room. She quickly gathered up the papers from the file and slid them back into their envelope. Then she carried them upstairs and locked them in her desk. With that out of the way, it only took her a few minutes to get ready to go out.

"I won't ask for specifics," Helen said as they got into the car. "I know you can't tell me anything, but I do hope you had a productive afternoon."

Bessie shrugged. "It didn't feel terribly productive, but that's why we've been given the case, because the solution isn't obvious."

Helen nodded. "I'll just wish you luck, then. I know you've done amazingly well so far."

"But you can't repeat that," Andrew told her as he pulled into the small car park for the restaurant.

"Of course not," Helen said with a small sigh.

"Everything we do is confidential for good reason," Andrew said as they walked towards the building.

"Yes, I know, but I'm awfully proud of my father and his team," Helen told him. "I want to shout from the rooftops about your success."

"It's difficult enough limiting the unit to a single case each month. If more people knew how successful we've been, I'd be flooded with even more cases," Andrew told her.

"Table for three," Bessie said to the man inside the restaurant.

He showed them to a small table in a relatively quiet corner.

"Is it always this busy?" Helen asked as he walked away.

Bessie looked around the dining room. There was only a single empty table. The rest were all occupied by groups of people at various stages of their meals. "We were lucky to get a table right away, actually. There's usually a wait."

"The food must be really good, then," Helen said.

"It's excellent," Bessie replied.

Over dinner, the trio talked about books they'd read in their childhoods. As she enjoyed her delicious meal, Bessie could feel some of the tension from the afternoon lifting.

"This case is really bothering you, isn't it?" Andrew asked her as they walked back towards the car after pudding.

She shrugged. Helen was a few paces away, so she quickly whispered a reply. "I did a quick read-through of all of the statements, and everyone sounded shocked and appalled by what had happened. I can almost understand being angry enough at someone to want him or her dead, but I can't understand killing innocent bystanders for any reason."

Andrew nodded. "It's hard to fathom. So is the idea that we might fail, but I think we all need to think about that reality."

"I thought some of our previous cases were difficult, but this one is by far the worst."

"Which is why I usually steer clear of anything that seems this difficult. I'm really sorry now that I picked this case."

"I haven't given up on it yet. Once I get home, I'm going to go back through the statements much more carefully. There must be things there that I missed."

"Let's get you home, then."

Helen was waiting at the car. They got in and Andrew drove them back to the beach. He insisted on walking Bessie back to her cottage and then checking that everything was as it should be before leaving her. She and Helen chatted in the kitchen while Andrew walked through Treoghe Bwaane.

"Are you working tomorrow?" Bessie asked her.

She nodded. "I'm afraid I'm working every day this fortnight. Getting Friday afternoon off is probably not going to happen. I hope we can do some sightseeing on the weekends, at least."

"We should plan on it. Maybe we'll have the case solved by the weekend."

"Is that likely?"

Bessie made a face. "Not at all. I think this might be the first one we don't solve."

"You'll solve it. I have confidence in you."

"We'll be off, then," Andrew said as he walked into the room. "I have a meeting tomorrow morning in Douglas, but I should be back in Laxey after lunch."

"Maybe I'll be ready to talk about the case by then," Bessie said. "I hope you have a good meeting," she added, burning with curiosity about his morning plans.

Helen grinned. "Meeting isn't the right word, though, is it, Dad?"

Andrew shrugged.

Helen looked at Bessie. "He's teaching a seminar to some of the constables and inspectors from the island's constabulary. Tomorrow is the first part, and then he'll do the second part next week."

"Goodness, how exciting for the island's constabulary!" Bessie exclaimed.

Andrew grinned. "I just hope most of them stay awake for the entire lecture."

Bessie and Helen both laughed.

"I'm sure it will be a fascinating seminar," Bessie said. "And you should be proud that you were asked to speak to them."

"I am, and I'm happy to share what I can with them, but I'd really rather be working on the case."

"Leave that with the rest of us for a few hours. You go and enjoy your talk."

Bessie hugged them both and then watched as they walked back to their holiday cottage. Helen waved as they went inside. Bessie shut her door and then made sure it was locked. Then she shut off the lights and turned off the phone's ringer before heading up the stairs. She unlocked her desk and pulled out the case file. Settling into a chair, she began to read again.

WHEN HER INTERNAL alarm woke her at two minutes after six the next morning, Bessie groaned and then shut her eyes tightly. "I don't have to get up," she reminded herself. "Andrew is in Douglas until after midday and no one else is going to be looking for me. I can sleep as late as I like."

Ten minutes later, having turned over half a dozen times, she gave up and got out of bed.

"It's your own fault," she told herself as she stared with tired eyes at her reflection. "You should have gone to bed at a reasonable hour."

When she'd sat down with the statements after dinner, she'd planned to read only a few of them, but instead she'd kept going, reading statement after statement until she'd read them all and it was well past her bedtime.

Feeling exhausted even after a shower, she got dressed and went down to start a pot of coffee brewing. The smell made her feel livelier, and once she'd had a few sips of the hot liquid, she decided she was almost awake. Toast with honey and strawberry jam was washed down with even more coffee. Then she grabbed an apple and headed out for her walk.

"I didn't need coffee," she muttered as she stepped out into a stiff, cool breeze. She marched down the beach, trying to eat her apple in spite of the wind that seemed to be doing its best to cover everything in sand. When she reached the stairs to Thie yn Traie, she turned around and headed for home.

"I'm wide awake now," she announced as she opened her door and stepped inside. A few minutes later, she was in her favourite chair in the sitting room, going back through the case file. An hour later, her phone rang.

"Hello?"

"I hate this case," Doona said.

Bessie laughed ruefully. "That makes two of us."

"I've read and reread every statement a dozen times, and I can't work out who was supposed to die or why."

"I've only read them half a dozen times, but, otherwise, I'm in the same place."

"John and I were wondering if you had plans for dinner

tonight. We'd love to talk about the case with you. We can invite Hugh and Andrew, too."

"Dinner tonight sounds good. I don't know what Andrew is doing, but I'm available."

"John and I were planning to have dinner with one of his friends from Manchester who was supposed to be coming across yesterday, which is why we didn't suggest it at the meeting," Doona explained. "But his plans got cancelled at the last minute."

"Six o'clock?" Bessie asked. "Do you want me to cook?"

"Six is good for us. John can bring something from the restaurant across from the station."

"What sort of food are they doing now?"

"That's a good question. I don't know. John mentioned that it had reopened, but I don't know if he knows what sort of food they're doing."

"If it's terrible, we can always have sandwiches. I have everything in for sandwiches."

Doona laughed. "It won't be that bad."

"I hope not."

"I'll ring Hugh and you can ring Andrew, okay?"

"He's in Douglas, teaching a seminar at the constabulary. I'll talk to him later, though."

"Ah, I knew that. John is there, too. I'll have him mention it to Andrew."

"That sounds good."

Doona sighed. "What else should we talk about? I really don't want to go back to the case file."

The pair chatted about a few mutual friends for a while.

"And now I really should get back to the file," Bessie said eventually. "I'll see you at six."

"See you at six."

Feeling restless now that she'd been disturbed, Bessie made herself some tea and then sat and nibbled on a biscuit while she watched the sea splashing against the sand. Then she went back into the sitting room and started reading again. She kept at it until someone knocked on her door just before midday.

"Helen, hello," she said, smiling at the woman on her doorstep.

"I know you're probably busy. I'm busy, too, but I'm taking a short lunch break and I thought maybe you could take one, too."

"I can," Bessie said quickly.

Helen grinned. "I brought sandwiches and crisps."

"How very kind of you."

The pair sat at Bessie's kitchen table and ate their sandwiches. Bessie supplied fizzy drinks and biscuits for pudding. They ate quickly and chatted happily for half an hour.

"And now I have to get back to work," Helen said with a sigh. "I don't know what you were planning to do for dinner tonight, but you'll have to do it without me. I have a dinner meeting with my team. They're all going out to a local restaurant. I get to ring them from here and talk to them on speaker while they eat their feast."

"It's a shame you have to miss the dinner."

Helen grinned. "Actually, they're going to a restaurant I don't like, so I don't mind in the slightest. I'm not sure what Dad will do, though."

"Hugh, John, and Doona are joining me for dinner to talk about the case. Your father will be more than welcome to join us."

"I'll let him know if I see him before you do."

Bessie nodded. "Thank you for lunch."

"Thank you for the company. Working from here is oddly isolating, even though I spend most of my days talking to other people."

Bessie watched her walk back to the holiday cottage and

then went back to work. She was taking even more notes when someone knocked on her door ninety minutes later.

"Hello," she greeted Andrew. "How was your seminar?"

"I think it went well. People seemed interested in what I had to say, and everyone seemed very enthusiastic at the end."

"Excellent."

"Unfortunately, I've no choice but to have dinner with the Chief Constable tonight, though. He was insistent that he needed to thank me properly."

"I'm sure you'll go somewhere very nice."

"We will, but I'd rather talk about the case with you and John and Doona and Hugh."

"Which you can do on Friday, anyway."

He chuckled. "But I often feel as if you and your friends find the key to the case when you have your smaller meetings."

"It isn't a meeting. We're having dinner together. Of course we'll talk about the case, but only informally."

Andrew nodded. "But making my excuses for dinner isn't the only reason I came over."

"Oh?"

"I found out some things about Kalynn Swanson."

Bessie frowned at his tone. "Maybe I'd better sit down."

"We may as well get comfortable. This might take a while."

Bessie led him into the sitting room and then sat down on the couch. He sat next to her.

"I should start by saying that everything is probably fine," he said. "I've no reason to believe that your friend's brother is in any danger."

"But?" Bessie asked.

"But I did learn some things that gave me pause."

Bessie frowned. "I should have offered you tea or coffee."

He shook his head. "I'm fine. I'm just trying to work out where to start."

"At the beginning?" Bessie suggested.

Andrew chuckled. "Yes, of course. Kalynn moved to Liverpool about three months ago. Prior to that, she had been living in London. She's forty-seven and single."

Bessie grabbed the notepad next to the phone and started taking notes.

Andrew named a large multinational corporation. "She works for them as an administrative assistant."

"Eugene said that Silvester told him that she worked in IT."

"She does work in the IT department, but I'm not sure I would consider that working in IT."

Bessie frowned. "What else did your friend discover?"

"It seems as if she's currently staying with friends in a flat near the restaurant where Silvester works. My friend watched the flat for a few hours one night and saw several people going in and out. Kalynn wasn't one of them."

"I assume Silvester wasn't, either."

"He was not. My friend also spent some time watching Silvester's flat. He didn't see anyone going in or out there."

"What else did he learn about Kalynn?"

"She doesn't have a criminal record. He reached out to a colleague in London. That colleague is going to speak to a few of Kalynn's former neighbours and see if he can learn more about the woman."

"Did she move to Liverpool for work?"

Andrew shrugged. "She was working for a different company in London, but she might have moved because she was offered the job in Liverpool. My friend in Liverpool didn't want to start asking questions, not until Silvester is actually reported missing."

"You said some things concerned you."

"That may have been overstating things a bit, but I'd prefer it if Kalynn were staying in a flat registered in her own name. My friend is fairly certain he's found where she's been staying, but he isn't positive. He didn't want to approach her employers under the circumstances."

"Is that all that worried you?"

"I would have been happier if my friend had been able to find Kalynn. Again, he didn't want to approach her employers, but he spent time watching her flat and walking around her neighbourhood and never saw her."

"So she may be missing, too," Bessie said.

"As of right now, we don't know that anyone is missing."

"It certainly sounds to me as if Silvester is missing."

"He might be, or he and Kalynn might have gone away for a few days and simply not told anyone."

"He didn't ring Marion on her birthday."

"Maybe, in the excitement of a new romance, he forgot."

"I suppose that's possible. What do you think happened?"

Andrew shrugged. "Right now, I'm not too worried. Silvester is an adult who has lived on his own for decades. Marion said that they didn't always speak every week, so maybe he regularly goes away and she simply isn't aware of his travels."

"Eugene said he rarely took time off."

"So maybe going away this week was something special that he did with his new girlfriend. Some of what Eugene said was mildly worrying, but nothing my friend found significantly increased my concern. Unless Marion wants to file a missing person report, there isn't much else we can do."

"Maybe your friend's colleague in London will learn something interesting."

"Maybe. He's supposed to try to speak to the neighbours later today."

"And Silvester is supposed to go back to work tomorrow.

If he doesn't turn up when he should, then I think Marion should definitely report him missing."

Andrew nodded. "I agree. It's one thing to miss ringing your sister on her birthday. Missing work, especially when you've been in a job for a long time and have always been reliable, is a much bigger concern."

Feeling as if they'd found out nothing useful, Bessie put the pen down and frowned at Andrew. "I'm worried about him. Something just feels off about all of this. Maybe his disappearance doesn't have anything to do with Kalynn, but I think he's definitely missing. And I think Kalynn is behind it, too."

"You can try to talk Marion into filing a report now, or you can wait until tomorrow and see if Silvester turns up for work."

Bessie sighed. "I know Marion doesn't want to do anything until tomorrow, but I'm going to ring her and try to persuade her otherwise."

"I'll go, then. I have some notes from today's seminar to go through. Based on the comments and questions that I got today, I want to make some changes to what I was planning to talk about next week. If I don't do that while everything is fresh in my mind, I'll forget what I wanted to change."

Bessie followed him to the door and then shut it behind him. Then she rang Marion. The pair talked for several minutes, but Bessie was unable to persuade her friend to file a report until Friday.

"He'll probably show up for work tomorrow, unbelievably hungover and grumpy," Marion said. "And he's going to be embarrassed enough that he missed my birthday. I don't want to make it even worse for him."

After the conversation, Bessie felt unsettled. She paced around her cottage until she started to feel annoyed with herself, and then went for another walk on the beach. When she got back to Treoghe Bwaane, she sat down with the case file again.

"This is a waste of time," she grumbled after half an hour.

Putting the paperwork to one side, she grabbed a thriller from the bookcase and started to read.

"This is more like it," she said a short while later. "Action, adventure, people racing around chasing shadows. This is much more exciting than that case file."

She read until just before the time her guests were due to arrive. She slid a bookmark into the book and then put it back on the shelf. Usually, she kept the book she was reading on the table next to her favourite chair, but she wasn't certain she wanted to finish that particular book.

"It's good," she argued with herself as she tidied up the kitchen. "But the pacing is off. It's all running around and chasing after whispered hints. No one has stopped to try to think if any of it makes sense or not. And none of it really makes sense."

She filled the kettle and then switched it on. Some of her guests would probably want tea. It hadn't boiled yet when someone knocked on the door.

"John, Doona, hello."

Bessie opened the door and then stood back to let John carry a large box into the cottage. Doona followed with a smaller box.

"Something smells good," Bessie said as she shut the door behind the pair.

"The restaurant across from the station is now doing what they call 'homemade comfort food,'" Doona told her.

"That sounds wonderful," Bessie said. "What did you get?"

Someone else knocked before John could answer. Bessie let Hugh in and then shut the door again.

"I'm starving," Hugh announced as he took off his coat.

"John was just going to tell us what he got from the restaurant," Bessie said.

John grinned. "I hope you like soups and stews and the like. I got a container of chicken and dumplings, one of chicken noodle soup, one of beef stew, and one of cottage pie."

"We'll need bowls rather than plates for most of that," Bessie said.

"We also got a box of various bread rolls, a container of mashed potatoes, and a container of roasted vegetables," Doona added.

"So plates and bowls," Bessie said. "And, actually, I have just the thing. Someone gave me a set of very small bowls years ago. I almost donated them to a charity shop, but I kept them in the end. I use one for porridge when I really don't want to eat it but I feel as if I must."

She opened a cupboard and then laughed. "John, you're a lot taller than I am. Can you get the box of bowls down? Since I only ever use one of them, I keep the rest of the set on the top shelf."

John got the box down and Bessie quickly unpacked eleven small bowls.

"They haven't been out of the box in years. Let me wash them quickly while you get everything out and ready to serve," Bessie said.

She ran washing-up water and then quickly worked her way through the bowls. Hugh dried them and then stacked them neatly on the counter. Doona got plates out of the cupboard and then set the table with knives, forks, and spoons.

"I forgot to mention pudding," Doona said as everyone began to help themselves to the various options.

"There's pudding?" Bessie asked, pausing before she added anything else to her plate.

Doona grinned. "We got brownies and chocolate-chip cookie bars."

"So maybe I don't want more than one bread roll," Bessie said. "The different varieties are very tempting, though."

A few minutes later, the foursome were in their seats around Bessie's table.

CHAPTER 10

"It's good," Doona said after a few bites.

"It is good," Hugh agreed.

"The beef stew is excellent," John said.

Bessie nodded. "I like the beef stew better than anything else, but it's all reasonably tasty."

"It actually does sort of taste homemade," Hugh said. "I'm pretty sure Grace's chicken and dumplings is better than this, though."

Doona nodded. "It's all good, but only the beef stew is really good. Still, I didn't have to cook any of it. We get lots of variety, and it wasn't all that expensive, either."

"And it doesn't really matter because we all know the restaurant will probably close next week," Hugh added.

They all laughed, but Hugh was probably correct. The restaurant across from the station seemed to change hands almost monthly. Bessie was always happy when they got a good meal from there, but she never expected the experience to be repeated.

"What shall we talk about?" Doona asked as Bessie tried her bread roll.

"I'm not sure we'll get anywhere talking about the case," Hugh replied. "It seems impossible, doesn't it?"

"And you were the one who was optimistic," John said.

Hugh shrugged. "I was, right up until I read the statements from the family and friends of the victims. I really thought there would be something there that we could dig further into, but I can't say I found much."

"Let's start at the beginning," Bessie said. "Let's talk about Dennis Baker and his girlfriend, Naomi."

"He was nearly twice her age," Doona said. "It seemed obvious from Naomi's statement that she was only interested in him for his money."

"And because she thought he might be able to help her career," Hugh added.

"Yes, of course," Doona said. "Because Dennis owned a number of very successful companies, and she thought he might give her a job at one of them once they broke up."

Bessie frowned. "It seemed odd to me that she was already planning for the end of their relationship."

"I saw it as evidence that she didn't care about Dennis in the slightest. She knew he was wealthy and successful, and she went after him in order to get what she could from him."

"I wonder if he knew that she was just using him," Hugh said.

"He must have suspected. She was much younger and, from the pictures, Dennis wasn't the most attractive man in the world," Doona said.

"He was dead in the pictures," John said. "I'm sure he was more attractive when he was alive."

Doona shrugged. "I can't see that it matters what Dennis knew or suspected. He was the victim."

"And Naomi was quite clear in her interview that she had lost more than just her boyfriend when he died," Bessie said. "According to her, he was also the key to her future success."

"I suspect she may have exaggerated some of that," John said. "She was just doing what she could to make it appear as if she didn't have a motive for his murder."

"I believed her, though," Doona said. "Even if she and Dennis were fighting, and no one has suggested that they were, I think Naomi was better off with him alive. All of his former girlfriends stated that he gave them very generous gifts when their relationships ended. If Naomi thought she was about to be dumped, she had to know that she was in line for a diamond bracelet or emerald earrings."

Bessie nodded. "She told Theodore that she and Dennis had been introduced to one another by a mutual friend. That friend was one of Dennis's former girlfriends, so Naomi probably did know what to expect when the relationship ended."

"And maybe she still had hopes that she was the one who would finally get the man to marry her," Doona added. "She said as much in her interview, but just sort of offhandedly."

John nodded. "I wish I could have seen her face when she said that. I think it might be interesting for Theodore to revisit that particular statement."

"Whether she was serious or not about marrying the man, did she have a motive for his murder?" Bessie asked.

"Maybe she said something about marriage to him at the party and he laughed in her face," Hugh suggested. "Maybe she just got so mad that she snapped and killed him."

"Do you think she was carrying the poison around with her, just in case she needed it?" Doona asked.

Hugh shrugged. "Maybe. We need to find someone with a motive for killing one of the people who died. I was just suggesting the only one I could think of for her."

"And it's a possibility. According to Naomi, they arrived at the party around quarter past seven. They got drinks from the bar near the entrance, which took a long time because that bar was busy. Then they walked around for a while, nodding and smiling at a few people who looked vaguely familiar."

"She claimed that she didn't actually know anyone else at the party," Doona said. "But that makes sense, because she and Dennis lived in Birmingham. She said that Dennis travelled to London for business meetings every few months, but that, before the party, she'd only ever been there as a tourist."

"And she said that it didn't seem as if Dennis knew anyone else, either," John added. "She said he nodded at a few people but didn't actually speak to anyone."

"And no one else at the party admitted to knowing him," Hugh said. "Which means if he was the intended victim, Naomi must have killed him."

"Let's talk about the fatal glass of wine, then," Bessie said. "Naomi said they walked around for a short while and then decided to get some food. After they'd filled plates, Dennis wanted another glass of wine. According to Naomi, while Dennis went to the bar, she took both plates and found a small table where they could stand and eat their food. He came back with a glass of dry white wine for himself and a glass of mulled wine for her."

"And while Naomi was nibbling on a tiny beef Wellington puff, Dennis took a sip of wine and then collapsed at her feet," Doona said.

"Naomi said that she started screaming and crying, but that it took at least a minute for anyone to pay any attention to her."

"I can't believe no one noticed that someone had fallen over," Hugh said.

"Maybe people noticed and didn't want to stare," Bessie suggested. "Maybe people thought that he was either ill or drunk and, either way, didn't want to get involved."

"The room was noisy," Doona added. "Many of the guests

commented that the band was good but very loud. People were talking and laughing and drinking. I did wonder if Naomi had shouted a bit louder if she might have saved two other lives, though."

"Before we move on to the next victim, does anyone have anything else to say about Dennis or Naomi?" John asked.

Bessie shook her head. "Naomi is at the bottom of my list of possible suspects. I know we only have her statement to work from, but it seemed as if she was much better off with Dennis alive than dead. Of course, I may change my mind on that when I find out what she's been doing since the murder."

Hugh nodded. "I understand why Andrew gives up the information in stages, but it's really frustrating to know that five years have passed since the murders and we don't know what has happened to any of the suspects in that time."

"We'll get that information tomorrow," Bessie said. "After we walk through a reconstruction."

"We're doing a reconstruction?" Doona asked.

Bessie nodded. "Jasper is going to set up the ballroom to replicate the party as closely as he can. I think that will really help. Right now, I'm struggling to understand how someone was able to add the poison to the bottle."

"That makes two of us," Doona said. "But, according to the police reports, anyone who went to the food table was close enough to the bottle in question to add something to it."

"They look close in the pictures, but I can't imagine being able to do something like that in a room full of people," Bessie replied.

"Bessie has put Naomi at the bottom of her list. Does anyone else want to say where they've put her?" John asked.

"She's at the bottom of my list, too," Doona said, "Even though I wasn't happy with the fact that she was just using poor Dennis."

"I hadn't really thought about it before now, but I'd put her at the bottom of my list, too," Hugh said.

John nodded. "I agree, at least until we find out what she's doing now."

"Which brings us to the unfortunately named Laurence Lawrence," Doona said.

"I can't imagine doing that to a baby," Hugh said. "I may be extra sensitive about names at the moment, though."

Bessie raised an eyebrow. "Oh?"

Hugh shrugged. "Grace and I are having trouble deciding what to name the baby, that's all. We've agreed on a name for a boy, but we can't seem to agree on a girl's name."

"You'll just have to hope for a boy, then," Doona said.

Hugh laughed. "Grace is convinced that it's a boy. She said she feels completely different this time than she did when she was pregnant with Aalish, but most of her mum friends have told her that it doesn't matter. She feels different because it's a different baby, regardless of gender."

"Would you like some suggestions for Manx names for the baby?" Bessie asked.

Hugh quickly shook his head. "We've already had too many suggestions. That's the problem. We have a short list of ten names that we both love. And before you say it, I know that isn't very short, but we had thirty-seven on the original list."

"You still have several months to make up your minds," Doona said.

"And you might want to wait until the baby arrives, anyway. My Amy was supposed to be called Angela, but when she arrived, Sue decided that she looked more like an Amy."

"And you didn't mind?" Bessie asked.

John chuckled. "I was actually delighted. One of my

former girlfriends was called Angela, and I didn't really fancy naming my child after her."

"Really?" Doona said. "You'll have to tell me about Angela one of these days."

John flushed. "We weren't together for long," he said.

Doona chuckled. "Later, darling," she said, patting his hand.

John looked as if he wanted to argue, but after a moment he looked down at his empty plate. "What about pudding?" he asked.

"I'm ready," Bessie said. "But I think I'd like to wash all the little bowls first."

"I'll do that," Hugh said. "And John can dry. You and Doona can sit and relax for five minutes."

"Or I can put away the food we didn't eat and get the puddings out," Doona said, getting to her feet. "Bessie, you relax."

"Or I can make tea," Bessie suggested. She started to get up, but Doona held up a hand.

"I'll make tea, too," she said as Hugh began clearing the table. "Does anyone want coffee?"

A few minutes later they were all sitting together with pudding and tea in front of them. They'd all decided to try both puddings. Bessie and Doona had small servings of each. John had taken more generous helpings, and Hugh's plate was nearly covered in large slices of each option.

Bessie took a bite of brownie and smiled. "Mine are better, but only slightly. These are really good, and I didn't have to lift a finger."

"The chocolate cookie bar is good, too," Doona said. "You can taste the vanilla."

Bessie tried a bite and then nodded. "These are better than mine," she admitted. "The next time I make them, I might try adding extra vanilla."

"Laurence Lawrence," John said a short while later. "Thirty years old and engaged to be married. He and June lived in Rugby in the same building, but not in the same flat."

Doona nodded. "June told Theodore that they were looking at houses, but that they hadn't found anything affordable, especially when they had to pay for a wedding, too."

"I read a few of the witness statements from people who claimed that they saw the pair arguing," Hugh said. "They were all very vague."

Bessie nodded. "Mostly, they said that June looked unhappy every time she spoke to Laurence, but June told Theodore that she'd been having a miserable time and had wanted to leave almost as soon as they'd arrived."

"She said she didn't feel comfortable in crowds," Doona said. "And she said that Laurence told her that it wasn't a crowd."

"Which wasn't very sympathetic of him," Bessie said.

"June said that they'd gone to London just to go to the party. Laurence was the one who'd been invited. He'd stayed at the hotel when he'd been sent to London for work, so he'd been surprised and excited when he'd been invited to the private event," Doona said.

John nodded. "And from what Theodore was able to find out, he really shouldn't have been invited. The invitations were only meant to go to guests who had stayed as private individuals, not guests whose stays had been paid for by their employers."

"Didn't June have an explanation for why it happened, though?" Doona asked, flipping through the pages in her notebook.

"Laurence had been supposed to stay at a different hotel, but someone made a mistake with the booking, or it had never actually been made or something," Bessie said. "June

THE LAWRENCE FILE

wasn't totally clear on exactly what went wrong. She just knew that Laurence ended up in London with nowhere to stay. So he checked himself into a luxury hotel using his own credit card and got his employer to reimburse him later."

Doona laughed. "That's either very smart or very risky."

"Probably both," Hugh said.

"It had happened back in May, and he was still working for the same employer, so it must have worked out okay," John said. "But with that in mind, you can understand why he was so excited to get invited to the party."

"And maybe why June was so overwhelmed. Most of the other guests were considerably wealthier and presumably more sophisticated," Doona said.

"So June was unhappy and wanted to leave, but Laurence was determined to stay and enjoy the party," John said. "According to June, they arrived around half seven. They'd taken the train to London and had only arrived at the hotel at half six. June said they went to their room and both got ready in a rush, and that she'd not been able to get her hair the way she wanted it before Laurence had insisted that they needed to go."

"No wonder she was unhappy," Bessie said.

"June said they got their first drinks from the bar near the door and then decided to get some food. They hadn't eaten on the train and then they'd been rushing, so she said they were both starving," Doona said.

"And then they stood at a table in the back of the room and ate. June said she went back for seconds and then thirds and that Laurence did the same," Hugh said.

"And by that time, she was feeling overwhelmed and wanted to go," Doona said. "Laurence suggested that they get another round of drinks and then try to find a quiet corner. They walked to the bar together, passing Naomi as they went. Dennis was right in front of them at the bar. He got his drink and then Laurence ordered for them."

Bessie looked at her notes. "Laurence asked for dry white wine for himself and sweet white wine for June."

"And then she very nearly drank the wrong one," Doona said. "She said they toasted and then she went to take a sip, but Laurence beat her to it. She said he took one sip and made a face and told her that they'd mixed up the glasses."

"Meanwhile, behind them, Dennis is falling to the ground," John said.

Doona nodded. "June and Laurence exchanged glasses, and June said she took a quick sip to make sure that Laurence was right. As she did so, Laurence drank from the other glass. A moment later, he fell to the ground."

"And June was so surprised that she just stood there and stared at him," Bessie said. "And again, you have to wonder what might have happened if she'd screamed."

"I hope that thought doesn't keep her up at night," Doona said quietly. "And I hope Naomi doesn't wonder if she could have saved lives if she'd acted faster. The killer is the guilty party here, and neither Naomi nor June should feel bad about how they reacted to what was happening."

"I didn't mean to suggest that they should," Bessie said quickly.

"And between them and the other victim's friends and family, they were able to stop anyone else from dying," John added. "At that point, no one knew what was happening. Everyone was just reacting to events in front of them."

"So do we think that June had a motive?" Hugh asked.

"Maybe," Bessie said. "She admitted in her interview that she knew that Laurence had already written a will with her as his sole beneficiary. I don't know that he had much to leave her, but if they were having problems, maybe she decided that she'd be better off with an inheritance than a husband."

"And that's the only reason why I put her higher on my list than Naomi," Doona said. "June had a motive, but I believed her when she talked about how shocked and devastated she was. She and Laurence had been together for three years, and she'd planned her entire future around him."

Bessie nodded. "I felt very sorry for her, and I couldn't imagine her killing anyone, let alone killing innocent strangers."

"I'm inclined to agree," John said. "It's always difficult to be certain whom to trust when we can only read their statements rather than meet them in person, but June seemed very believable."

"Actually, I'm not sure I believed her," Hugh said. "I thought some of her answers sounded almost too perfect. To me, either she was devastated but surprisingly coherent, or she'd practiced her answers."

Bessie frowned. "I didn't get that impression, but now I want to reread her statement."

Hugh grinned. "Why don't you do that while I get myself a bit more chocolate-chip cookie bar?" he suggested.

Everyone laughed.

"Did you really doubt June's words, or do you just want more pudding?" Doona asked.

"Both," Hugh said.

"Let's take a short break," Bessie suggested. "I want more tea, and I won't object to another small piece of brownie, but mostly I want to read June's statement again."

"I think we all do," John said.

CHAPTER 11

Twenty minutes later, Bessie looked up from June's statement. While she and the others had been reading, Hugh had made tea and served everyone extra pudding. Bessie's brownie piece was larger than she would have cut for herself, but she didn't complain.

"What do you think?" Hugh asked.

"I can see what you mean," Bessie said. "I still don't think she's the killer, but you're right. She does seem more coherent than maybe she should have been under the circumstances."

"I'm keeping her right where I had her," Doona said after a bite of cookie bar. "Above Naomi, but below the other three."

"Are we ready to talk about them now, then?" John asked.

"I'm not even sure where to start with them," Bessie said. "They're an interesting group of people."

"They must be more likely suspects because the victim they knew got the first glass of wine from the bottle," Hugh said.

Bessie nodded. "It certainly seems that way. Let's walk

THE LAWRENCE FILE

through their evening. They arrived at the party right at seven."

"And they were first in line at the bar by the door," Hugh said.

"They were celebrating Christmas and Myra's divorce," Doona said.

"But Lucy and Olga didn't really know Myra," John added. "She was Brenda's sister, but they both said they'd barely ever spoken to her before the night of the party."

"And Myra said that was because her ex-husband hadn't wanted her to spend much time with her sister," Doona said.

Bessie frowned. "Or anyone else, from what Myra said."

Hugh nodded. "Myra said the Christmas party was the first party she'd been to in years, and that she never would have been allowed to attend if she'd still been married."

"It was Brenda who'd received the invitation," John said. "When she'd come to London for the engagement party, she'd stayed in a room with Olga."

"And Lucy stayed in a room with a different friend, one who was safely back in Guernsey on the night of the Christmas party," Hugh said.

John nodded. "Myra said that Brenda had insisted that she come to the party, that Brenda was doing everything in her power to drag her out at every opportunity."

"Which didn't agree with what Lucy and Olga said," Bessie said. "They both said that Brenda had told them that Myra had seen the party invitation and had demanded that Brenda take her. They said that Brenda had been planning to invite their other friend to join them, but that Brenda hadn't wanted to upset Myra any further. According to Olga and Lucy, Myra had been crushed when her husband had asked for a divorce."

"Except Myra told the police that she was the one who'd asked for the divorce," Bessie said. "And she told the police

123

that she was nothing but relieved that her marriage was over. She said she had been really excited when her sister had invited her to London for the Christmas party. According to her, Brenda had promised her that they'd spend the entire weekend celebrating the divorce."

"That was before Myra knew that Olga and Lucy were also going to be at the party," Doona said.

"Yeah," Hugh said. "Myra didn't sound very happy about them being there, really."

"To be fair, she didn't really know them. If she'd been expecting to celebrate her divorce with her sister, I can understand her being disappointed when two more people showed up," Doona said.

"But both Olga and Lucy seemed to think that Myra knew they were going to be there. They said that Brenda had talked about all sorts of plans for the four of them and that they both assumed that Myra was part of the planning process, even though neither of them had ever actually spoken to her."

"And Myra said that Brenda had told her to leave everything to her and that she'd plan the perfect weekend," Doona said. "Except I couldn't stop thinking that Myra was lying."

Bessie nodded. "I didn't believe her, either, but I can't tell you why."

"The worst part with this group was trying to work out where everyone was all the time," Doona said.

"They all agreed that they'd arrived at seven and been first in line at the bar," Hugh said. "But then things got fuzzy."

"Myra said she stayed with her sister while Olga and Lucy wandered off," Bessie said, reading from her notes.

"And Olga said that she finished her first drink and then went to the loo," Doona said. "When she got back to the party, Lucy was flirting with one of the waiters while Myra and Brenda had gone to get food."

"And then Olga stopped to talk to someone she thought she knew who turned out to be a total stranger," Doona said. "But that stranger was friendly enough, because they talked for around twenty minutes."

Bessie shook her head. "And from what Lucy said, she talked to the waiter for about the same amount of time."

"I'm surprised he didn't get fired," Doona muttered.

"Eventually, not long before eight, they all reunited near the food table," Doona said. "And then they all got in the queue for food."

"And all three women mentioned standing near the bar while they were waiting, which means they all had the opportunity to add the poison to the bottle of wine," Doona said.

"But then they got food and walked back across the room," Bessie said. "If I'd just put poison in a wine bottle, hoping to kill someone, I wouldn't just walk away."

"As soon as they found somewhere to stand, though, Myra went and got drinks for everyone," Doona said.

"And she walked all the way back to the bar near the food because it was the quietest," Bessie said. "I wonder if that was her idea or if someone else in the group suggested it."

"They were all asked to repeat the conversation, and none of the accounts agreed," John said. "Myra even said that Brenda suggested that she go to the bar at the back of the room because there were queues everywhere else."

"Lucy and Olga were both insistent that Myra offered to get drinks and that she was the one who decided which bar to go to," Bessie said.

"I got the feeling that they both wanted to suggest that Myra put the poison in the bottle when she went back for the drinks, but that they didn't want to come right out and accuse their friend's sister of murder."

"Even though it was their friend who died," Bessie said.

"And it is possible that Myra did put the poison in the wine when she went back for the drinks," John said. "But it's also possible that one of the others did it while they were queuing for food. I'm inclined to believe Myra about who suggested which bar she should go to. I suspect that if Brenda hadn't made the suggestion, one of the other women might have."

"And we'd know who the killer was," Hugh said.

John shrugged. "Maybe. I'm just keeping all of the possibilities on the table, really. Just because Myra went and got the drinks, doesn't mean that she put the poison in the bottle."

"If it were that easy, Theodore would have arrested her years ago," Bessie said.

"Exactly," John said. "As it was, he couldn't find a motive for Myra."

"Before we get to that, let's talk about what happened at the bar," Bessie said. "Myra went over and ordered two glasses of mulled wine, a gin and tonic, and a glass of dry white wine. The bartender had a pile of small trays, so he put the drinks on a tray and then handed it to Myra."

"And she carried it back to her sister and their friends," John said.

"They toasted to Christmas and then they all drank," Doona said. "Myra said that while she was sipping her mulled wine, she noticed some commotion near the bar at the back of the room. Before she could even say anything, though, Brenda collapsed."

"Olga said much the same thing," Hugh said. "Lucy was facing the wrong way to see what was happening at the back of the room. She saw Brenda fall before she realised that something was wrong elsewhere."

"Myra kept insisting that she blamed herself, that she should have gone to a different bar or that she should have tasted the wine herself before she let her sister drink it," Doona said.

"Which is silly," Hugh said. "No one taste-tests drinks for other adults."

Bessie nodded. "She'd just lost her sister under horrific circumstances. I can understand her not making sense."

"She said they'd always been very close," Doona said.

"And Lucy and Olga said otherwise," Hugh said.

John frowned. "They both said that Brenda only tolerated her sister out of a sense of obligation and that she'd been quite happy when Myra had been married to a man who did his best to keep the sisters apart."

"If that's true, it's quite sad," Doona said.

"If it's true, does that give Myra a motive for her sister's murder?" Bessie asked.

"They were at a party together," Hugh said. "That suggests that they got along, at least a little bit."

Bessie nodded. "And according to Myra, she and Brenda had been spending a lot of time together since her divorce. If Brenda had only been doing what she felt obliged to do, surely she would have done less than she did."

"So what did you all think of Olga and Lucy?" Hugh asked.

Bessie frowned. "I didn't care for either of them, but I can't really explain why."

"It sounded as if Lucy spent a lot of the party flirting with every man she met," Doona said. "And that included the bartender at the back of the room."

"Joseph remembered her," John said. "He said she spent a lot of time hanging on the bar, chatting, while the others were in the queue for food. Then, when they got to the front of the queue, she went and joined them."

"Which would have annoyed me if I'd been in the queue behind her," Doona said.

Bessie nodded. "It is a bit rude."

"But does that make her more or less likely as the killer?" Doona asked. "On the one hand, she had plenty of time to add something to the wine bottle, but she also drew attention to herself by hanging around the bar for so long. If I were going to poison someone, I'd be trying to be as inconspicuous as possible."

"Good to know," John said with a grin.

Doona laughed. "You know what I mean."

"If Myra had been the one murdered, I'd suspect Olga," Hugh said. "She and Lucy both seemed to dislike Myra, but Olga especially didn't care for her."

Bessie nodded. "They both said that Brenda didn't really want to invite Myra, but Olga went so far as to say that she wished that Myra had been the one to die."

Doona winced. "I suppose I can understand her feeling that way. She'd just lost a dear friend, but it was still hard to read."

"Let's talk about motives," John said. "Lucy and Olga both disliked Myra, but they both seemed very fond of Brenda."

"But they did all work together, and one of them – I think it was Lucy – did admit that they were often in competition for clients," Bessie said.

John nodded. "So maybe the friendship was more superficial than it appeared."

"They both said that Brenda was good at her job," Doona said. "I'd like to hear more about that, actually. No one asked them for details."

"I'd like to know if either of them had recently lost a client or two to Brenda," Bessie said. "It isn't much of a motive, but it's something."

"Myra didn't have much of a motive," Doona said. "At least not according to Myra."

"She claimed that she and Brenda were close," Bessie said. "The other two women didn't agree."

"So maybe they hated one another and Myra had been waiting years for a chance to kill her," Hugh said.

"Assuming she didn't hate her sister, Myra didn't have an obvious motive. Their parents had died years earlier and everything they'd left had been split fifty-fifty between the sisters. From what she said, I got the feeling that Myra was better off financially than Brenda. It doesn't seem as if Myra would have killed her for money."

"We need to find out what happened to Brenda's money," Bessie said. "I'd like to know the contents of the wills of all three victims, really."

John nodded. "I hope that information is included with the updates we're going to get tomorrow."

"By all accounts, the sisters were getting along fine on the night of the party," Hugh said. "Even Lucy and Olga said as much."

"But they weren't with the sisters the entire time," Doona said. "Maybe Brenda and Myra had a huge fight while Lucy and Olga were busy elsewhere."

"And then made up by the time the other two rejoined them?" Hugh asked.

"Maybe they agreed to pretend that they were getting along until after the party," Doona said.

"So we have Naomi at the bottom of every list, with June just above her. Where do Brenda, Lucy, and Olga go on your lists?" John asked.

Bessie thought for a minute. "The problem with this case is trying to imagine anyone killing innocent bystanders. I didn't care for Olga or Lucy, but it's difficult to imagine either of them being that evil."

"I agree with Bessie, but if I have to rank them, then I'd

put Olga at the top of the list," Doona said. "Maybe she was trying to kill Myra and got it wrong."

"But Myra had been drinking mulled wine all evening," Hugh said.

Doona shrugged. "So maybe she was so angry that Brenda had included Myra in their evening that she decided to get rid of Brenda."

"Or maybe there was something going on at work," Bessie said thoughtfully. "I think Theodore needs to dig more into that."

John nodded. "There may be more in the updates, of course, but he didn't ask as many questions about that as I would have."

"Who comes after Olga on your list?" Hugh asked Doona.

"Lucy, and then Myra," Doona replied. "Myra seemed really upset about losing her sister. And the same possible work-related motive applies to Lucy as much as Olga."

Bessie looked up from her notes. "I'd put them in the same order. I think Theodore needs to look more closely at Olga and Lucy."

"I'm not sure I agree," John said. "I do think they both need a closer look, but if one of them was the killer, she took a huge risk putting the poison in the bottle and then walking away. If it had taken Myra just a few minutes longer to get the drinks, Brenda would have known not to drink the wine."

"Maybe that was a risk she was prepared to take," Bessie said thoughtfully. "Maybe one of them wanted Brenda gone but wasn't in a particular hurry to kill her. Maybe this was just an attempt and whoever was behind it was prepared to keep trying."

"After all of that, I think we need to look more closely at the rest of the guests again," Hugh said with a sigh.

"I intend to go through all of the statements I haven't already read," Bessie said.

John nodded. "I think we all do."

"It's frustrating," Doona said. "I don't want to wait until tomorrow to find out where everyone is now."

"I'd be more frustrated if I didn't have close to a hundred other statements to read," Bessie said.

Doona laughed. "Fair point. Okay, I won't complain until after I've read all of the other statements."

"What else do we need to talk about tonight?" Bessie asked.

John shrugged. "I'm not sure there is anything else to discuss. We have a few things that we want more information about, but that information might be in the updates. I don't think we have anything to send back to Theodore yet, really."

"Let's hope we'll have something after tomorrow," Doona said. "If we can't come up with any new questions, we can't solve the case."

As John got up and started to clear away the pudding plates, Bessie cleared her throat.

"I don't think any of you ever met Silvester Crellin," she said.

She got blank stares from all of her friends.

"He and his sister are from Lonan," she explained. "And he's missing."

"From Lonan?" John asked, sitting back down at the table and pulling out his notebook.

"No, from Liverpool. He moved across fifteen years ago, after his mother passed away."

"How do you know he's missing?" Doona asked as she stood up. While Bessie replied, Doona continued the job that John had been doing.

"His sister, Marion, rang me. She'd spoken to Silvester on Saturday last week but hadn't heard from him since."

Hugh frowned. "Did they speak daily, then? They are both adults, aren't they?"

"They're both in their sixties, and no, they didn't usually speak every day, but Monday was Marion's birthday. Silvester always rang on her birthday," Bessie explained.

"Has she reported him missing?" John asked.

Bessie shook her head. "She doesn't want to do that, just in case he's simply having a holiday and forgot her birthday."

"So she rang you?" Doona asked.

Bessie flushed. "She seemed to think that now that I'm part of a cold case unit, I'm an expert on finding missing people."

Everyone chuckled.

"If she doesn't want to report him missing, then there isn't much the police can do," John said.

"I know, and Andrew said the same, but it's really bothering me. I can't help but feel as if something awful has happened to the man," Bessie replied.

"Tell me everything," John said.

While Doona and Hugh did the washing-up, Bessie told John everything she could about Silvester's disappearance.

"So if he doesn't turn up for work tomorrow, his sister is going to report him missing?" John checked when she was finished.

"That's what Marion said when we last spoke, anyway."

"I think that's smart. It does seem possible that Silvester went away with his new girlfriend and simply forgot his sister's birthday, but if he doesn't return to work tomorrow, I'll be more concerned."

"If Marion doesn't report him missing, Eugene might," Bessie said. "He seemed more worried than Marion when we spoke."

"I don't think there is anything else you can do," John said as he put his notebook away. "If you think it would help, I'd be happy to be the one who takes Marion's report, but it would probably be better if the report was made in Liverpool by Silvester's employer."

"I'm sure it would help if you were the one to talk to Marion. I think she'd feel more comfortable talking to someone that she knows I know. I can't imagine she talks to police inspectors very often."

"What time is Silvester due at work?"

Bessie shrugged. "I didn't think to ask."

"Ring me if you hear from Marion and she wants to make a report," John said. "I can go and talk to her, even if all that I do is tell her to have the report made in Liverpool."

Bessie smiled. "Thank you."

"I haven't done anything yet."

"'But you will, and that makes me feel much better."

John pulled her into a hug. "You know that talking to her is just part of my job."

"Except you have an entire team of people who could talk to her. You don't have to go out of your way to do it yourself."

"I'd do it," Hugh said. "If John hadn't already offered."

Bessie gave Hugh a hug. "I know you would," she said. "And I know you're both offering because we're friends. I really appreciate it."

"I'm not offering," Doona said.

They all laughed.

Bessie insisted on sending all of the extra food home with Hugh. Doona took what little was left of both puddings.

"We should get food from there again soon," Bessie said as her friends headed for the door. "If we don't hurry, we probably won't get a second chance."

"Maybe I'll go there before I head to Ramsey tomorrow,"

Hugh said. "I can get a tray of brownies and another cookie bar and bring them to the Seaview. They were much nicer than what we were given there yesterday."

"Maybe everyone has made up and we'll get something better tomorrow," Doona said.

"We won't have time for treats anyway, not if we're doing the reconstruction," Bessie said.

"We'll find time for a tea break," Hugh said. "We always do."

Bessie laughed, and then opened the door for the trio. She watched as Doona and John got into his car. Hugh stopped to put the leftover food into his boot, so John was already driving away as Hugh got into his car. He gave Bessie a huge wave as he drove out of the parking area.

Smiling to herself, Bessie shut the door and then locked it. After checking that everything was the way she wanted it, she gathered all of the paperwork and went up the stairs. After getting ready for bed, she crawled under the duvet with a small stack of statements from the pile that she hadn't already read. She found herself yawning after the first one.

"Sleep is important, too," she reminded herself as she put the statements on her bedside table. After switching off the light, she rolled over and shut her eyes.

I really hope Silvester comes to work tomorrow, was her last thought before she fell asleep.

CHAPTER 12

As Bessie walked along the sand the next morning, she felt as if she wanted to keep going forever. Outside, enjoying the sea air, she could momentarily forget about Silvester and Marion and the three dead partygoers and just enjoy her beautiful island home. She walked until she'd nearly reached the row of new houses and then reluctantly turned back towards home.

She was only a few paces away from her front door when she heard someone call her name.

"Helen, good morning," she said as she turned around and saw the woman behind her.

"Good morning. You're just back from your walk, then? I was going to join you, but I'm afraid I had a bit of a lie-in," Helen replied.

"I don't mind walking for a bit longer if you want to walk a short distance."

Helen nodded. "We can just walk to those rickety-looking stairs and back. That will be enough to wake me up properly and get me ready for my day."

"The stairs do look quite rickety," Bessie said as the pair

fell into step together. "And they're quite dangerous, too. I fell down them once, although I should say that I was pushed down them."

"My goodness. How dreadful. I hope the fall didn't cause any serious damage."

"I was very lucky. I fell onto soft sand. I had the wind knocked out of me, but otherwise I was fine."

"That is lucky. I can't imagine I'll ever have a reason to climb those stairs, but if I do, I'll be extra careful."

"If Mary's health improves, I'm sure she'd enjoy meeting you. Having said that, if you do visit, you can always just drive around to the front door."

Helen laughed. "I probably would, if only because I've never seen the front of the building. It looks enormous and quite unwelcoming from here."

"I think it's a very cold house, but Mary seems to love it. It is smaller and cozier than their house in Douglas, at least."

"They have a larger house in Douglas?"

"It's been on the market for years, but I believe they've decided to try turning it into an event centre rather than sell it."

"Does the island need an event centre?"

Bessie shrugged. "I'm the wrong person to ask. I didn't think the island needed a party planner, but their daughter, Elizabeth, managed to build a very successful business before she suddenly had to leave the island."

"If she's a party planner, then she probably has a much better idea of what the island needs in terms of event space. And, I suppose, if the house is just sitting empty for now, that it makes sense to try to find a use for it."

"Yes, although, knowing Elizabeth, she'll want to pour thousands of pounds into renovations before she does anything else."

"But renovating and decorating are such wonderful

things," Helen exclaimed. "I got incredibly excited when I bought my last flat. It was the first time I'd ever bought anything on my own, and I had all sorts of wonderful ideas for every single room."

"And did you do them all?"

Helen made a face. "I managed a few of them, but the sensible side of me stepped in before I started taking down walls."

"That does sound as if it would be a lot of work."

"It would have been, and I didn't really have the budget for it. I did paint every room, and I put in new flooring in most of them. It's the first place I've lived in a long time that's truly felt as if it was home."

"My cottage is home, and it has felt that way since the first time I saw it."

"I can't imagine how wonderful that must be."

"It is wonderful," Bessie agreed. "But I sometimes wonder what might have happened to me if I hadn't felt so settled in my little cottage. There was another man who asked me to marry him."

"Oh? But you turned him down? Did you love him?"

Bessie sighed. "I didn't allow myself to think about loving him. He lived in Australia, and I wasn't prepared to move halfway around the world for him. I suppose that means I didn't love him, doesn't it?"

"Probably."

"There was a time when I considered moving back to the US as well."

"Oh? You did tell me that you'd grown up there."

"Yes, and once I was on my own, I considered moving back there. My sister was still there, you see, and she'd begun having children. She offered to pay my passage if I wanted to return. She suggested that I could act as nanny to her children while they were very small."

"Were you interested in the job?"

Bessie laughed. "I don't know. At the time, I rather assumed that I'd be nanny to a baby or two and then, when they were a bit older, I'd get married and start having babies myself. As it happened, my sister had ten children, so if I'd promised to stay and look after all of her babies, I'd have been stuck in that job for a long time."

"Ten children? I can't even imagine."

"Neither can I."

"But you decided not to take the job. Why?"

"I was just starting to feel settled on the island. The idea of moving to the other side of the world again just felt as if it would be too much to endure at that point. My little cottage already felt too much like home, I suppose."

They'd reached Thie yn Traie. Helen stopped to look up at the mansion above them.

"When I was younger, I always assumed that the people who live in such big, beautiful homes must be happy all the time," she said.

"It's very true that money doesn't buy happiness."

"Yes, now I know that's true."

"Would you like to come in for a cuppa?" Bessie asked as they got close to Treoghe Bwaane.

Helen shook her head. "I have a meeting in ten minutes, and then about a dozen emails to send. Thank you for the walk, though."

"It was my pleasure."

Bessie spent the rest of her morning going through the statements she hadn't read before. While she made a few notes about people who caught her attention for one reason or another, by the time she'd finished the pile, she found herself agreeing with the conclusion that John and Doona had reached. Aside from Bill and Dorothy Hughes, there didn't seem to be anyone in the pile who warranted a second look.

"Just the staff to go," she muttered as she glanced at the clock. Somehow it was midday. Bessie's stomach rumbled loudly as she realised that the entire morning had gone.

Wondering where Andrew had been all morning, Bessie got up and stretched. "Lunch," she muttered as she blinked several times. Someone knocked on her door before she'd moved from the table.

Unsure of who it might be, she quickly gathered up all of the papers on the table and shoved them into their envelope. Then she opened the door.

"Good morning, even though it's afternoon," Andrew said. "I'm sorry that I rather abandoned you this morning."

"I spent the morning with the other fifty party guests," Bessie told him. "It wasn't productive, but it needed doing."

"I spent most of the morning on the telephone with my solicitor, but that's a story for another time," Andrew replied. "I thought maybe we could get lunch in Ramsey before the meeting, but if you're busy I can leave you working and go and have lunch with Helen."

Bessie frowned. "Surely you'd enjoy having lunch with your daughter."

"I would if she weren't so busy working. I doubt she'll take a lunch break. She'll probably make herself a sandwich and eat in between meetings."

"In that case, let's go and get lunch in Ramsey," Bessie said. "I really don't want to read the other forty-whatever statements right now. My brain is mush after this morning's work."

"I need ten minutes to tell Helen our plans and then get everything I need for the meeting into my briefcase."

"I'll be ready in ten minutes, then."

She was standing next to Andrew's hire car when he emerged from his cottage a short while later.

"Where shall we go?" he asked as he pulled out of the parking area.

Bessie suggested a small café that she knew did good food. "I haven't been there in ages. They may have changed hands half a dozen times since my last visit, but the food used to be very good."

The café still had the same owners, and the food was still good. They headed for the Seaview a few minutes early.

"I can't wait to see what Jasper has done with the ballroom," Bessie said. "I just hope the reconstruction helps."

"It can't hurt. At this point, I'm about ready to try anything."

Bessie nodded. "It is a very frustrating case."

When they walked into the Seaview a few minutes later, Jasper greeted them with a smile.

"I have everything set up for you," he said. "Including tea and coffee and a selection of breakfast pastries. The pastry chef came in very early this morning and started creating all sorts of new things that he wants to add to the menu. I know he was just trying to annoy the head chef, but the end result was that we were able to offer guests free samples at breakfast this morning. They were all very excited, and we had enough left over for your meeting."

"Breakfast pastries? How lovely," Bessie said.

"Croissants, chocolate croissants, a variety of muffins, cinnamon rolls, and Danishes in apple, pear, and peach," Jasper said. "I think that was everything."

Bessie sighed. "I can't possibly try them all."

"Maybe we can share a few of them," Andrew suggested.

"They're pastries in miniature," Jasper added. "Tiny, delicate, and delicious, at least according to the pastry chef."

"Lovely," Bessie said.

Jasper walked with them down the corridor to the conference room. "I set up your food table where the food table was in your floor plan," he told them as he opened the door. "And the tea and coffee are behind the bar nearest to the door."

Bessie looked around the room. Small screens had been erected around the room to mark the dimensions of the party space. There were three bars, each in the appropriate place, and a stage for the band. Tape marked out the space for the dance floor.

"There is a case of empty bottles on the bar at the back of the room," Jasper told them. "I've also put a box of wine glasses back there. From what I've seen, I'm pretty certain I know what case you're working on, so I thought those things might be helpful."

Andrew nodded. "They will be very helpful. Thank you."

There were a number of small tables near the food table. Bessie walked back and stood next to one of them.

"Are these the correct height?" she asked.

Jasper nodded. "The floor plan had specifics on everything."

She looked at Andrew. "We would have just marked everything with tape and tried to use our imaginations."

"You've done a wonderful job here," Andrew told Jasper. "I can't tell you how much we appreciate it."

"I'm happy to help in any small way. The work that you are doing is very important, and this particular case matters to me a great deal."

"Oh?" Andrew said.

"I know the owners of that hotel. The hospitality world is a lot smaller than most people realise. The murders nearly destroyed their business. It's been five years and they're still struggling to recover. The scary part is that such a thing could happen anywhere. I'm always anxious before big events, but prior to what happened there, I'd never worried that someone might add poison to a bottle of wine and kill some of the guests."

Bessie gave him a hug. "Fortunately, such incidents are few and far between."

"And now your unit is considering the case. Once you've solved it, maybe people will start to forget what happened."

"There's no guarantee that we'll solve it," Bessie said quickly.

"I have confidence in you," Jasper said brightly. He gave Bessie another hug and then turned and walked out of the room.

Andrew looked at Bessie. "This is even better than I imagined it could be."

"It's wonderful, but I don't know if it will help."

"The pastries look good, at least."

Bessie chuckled and then looked over at the food tables. The pastries did look good, actually.

"We may as well try a few while we're waiting," Andrew suggested. "We didn't have pudding with lunch, after all."

They were standing at a table in the back of the room when John and Doona arrived.

"This is wonderful," Doona said as she looked around the room. "I can already visualise things more clearly."

She and John were walking around the room when Hugh arrived. He was filling a plate with pastries when Harry and Charles walked into the ballroom.

"Someone worked hard in here," Charles said.

"Jasper probably had his entire event team in here," Bessie said. "He knows the owners of the hotel in London, so he feels personally involved."

"You told him what case we're working on?" Harry asked Andrew.

"No, but he guessed from the floor plan," Andrew

explained. "I knew there was a risk that he might, even though I covered up all of the identifying information, but I trust Jasper."

"You should," Bessie said.

"So where do we start?" Doona asked.

"I think we need to set up the bar," Andrew said. He opened his briefcase and took out his case file. When he pulled out the relevant pictures, he set them on top of the table.

"I'll just grab a few more pastries," Hugh said quietly as he moved towards the food table.

"Charles, why don't you go behind the bar and pretend to be Joseph. We have his statement and the pictures of how the bottles were arranged," he said.

Bessie watched as Charles and Andrew set bottles behind the bar and onto the table next to it. Joseph had stated that the second table was necessary for extra bottles and, now that Bessie could see exactly how the bar had been set up, she could understand what he meant.

Andrew used a red marker to make a large "X" on the cork of one of the bottles. Then he marked the bottle's label as well.

"So that's the one with the poison," Harry said.

"Not yet it isn't," Andrew told him. "But it's going to be."

Once the bar was ready, they all walked to the door.

"Let's start with the four women," Andrew suggested. "They arrived first. Let's walk through their evening, right up until the murders. Then we'll do the same with the other two victims."

Bessie pulled out her notes. "They walked in just after seven and immediately stopped at the first bar," she said.

"Doona, Bessie, John, and Hugh, can you pretend to be the four women, please?" Andrew asked.

They mimed getting drinks from an imaginary bartender and then turned and walked towards the centre of the room.

"And then Olga went to the loo," Bessie said.

"I'll be Olga," Doona said, taking a few steps away.

"And when she came back, Lucy was flirting with a waiter," Bessie continued. "But why did she walk away from Myra and Brenda?"

Harry frowned. "I remember her saying that she finished her drink and then wandered away, but I don't remember her saying why she'd left the other two."

"Maybe she was going to the loo but got distracted by the waiter," Hugh suggested.

"Maybe, but she needs to be asked," Andrew said.

"And Myra needs to be asked," Bessie added. "I'm curious what she'll have to say on the subject."

"I'll be the waiter," Charles offered.

He walked a few steps away.

"I'll be Lucy," Hugh said after a moment. He joined Charles, while Bessie and John stayed where they were.

"And then, after some time passed, they reunited," Andrew said. "And decided to get food."

The foursome walked towards the food table together.

"I can see now how the queue would have taken them right up against the overflow bar table," Bessie said. "And the bottles are in a single line, so it would have been pretty simple for someone who knew what they were looking for to spot the right bottle."

"But how easy would it have been for them to add poison to the bottle?" Doona asked.

"Let's try it," Andrew said. "Pretend there is a long queue in front of you and stand along the side of the bar table."

They moved into position.

"It's a pretty small table," Bessie said. "Are the dimensions correct?"

Andrew checked his notes. "They are."

"I can easily reach over and help myself to some wine," Doona said with a laugh.

"Lucy, you're supposed to be flirting with the bartender," Andrew reminded Hugh.

Charles went back behind the bar and grinned at Hugh. "You look lovely tonight," he said.

Hugh laughed. "It's a new dress."

As they were chatting, Bessie reached over and took the cork out of the bottle with the red X. Then she pretended to add something to the bottle before putting the cork back into the bottle upside down.

"I don't think we're getting anywhere," Hugh said.

"Except while you were talking to Joseph, someone poisoned the wine," Andrew said, nodding towards the bottle on the table.

"I only looked away for a second," Hugh protested.

"And I thought I was keeping watch on the bottles, but I missed it," Charles admitted.

"I saw what happened, but I was watching the wine bottle, not people. No one would have been watching the bottle during the party," Harry said.

"So any one of the four women could have put the poison in the bottle while they were waiting for their turn at the food table," Andrew concluded.

"Which means anyone who got food could have done it," Harry added.

"Which means we aren't any closer to working things out," Doona sighed.

"Let's keep going," Andrew suggested. "Once we've walked through it all, we'll talk about where everyone is now."

"So we get our food and we walk back to the middle of the room," Doona said. "And then we send Myra for drinks."

"Why Myra?" Bessie asked.

"Didn't Lucy say she offered?" Doona said.

"Maybe. Maybe they should all be asked that again, too," Bessie suggested.

Andrew made a note.

"And then Myra came back, and they all took their drinks, and Brenda fell to the ground," Andrew said.

They walked through it, leaving Bessie feeling sad.

"And now we need to do the same for the other two victims," Andrew said.

By the time those were done, Andrew had a short list of questions for Theodore.

"I think we need a break," he said as Harry, who'd been standing in for Dennis, slowly got back to his feet. "Let's all get tea or coffee and some pastries and sit and talk about the weather or something for a few minutes."

"And then we'll talk about where everyone is now?" Harry asked.

Andrew nodded. "I need tea and something sweet first, though."

CHAPTER 13

※

A short while later, the group took seats around a long table that Jasper had placed just outside of the re-created party space.

"I feel as if I learned a lot but that we aren't any further ahead," Charles said as Bessie sipped her tea.

Andrew nodded. "It's easier to picture the scene, and easier to believe that anyone who went to the food table could have poisoned the wine, but I don't think we got any closer to working out who actually did it."

"In the past we've learned a lot from finding out where people are now," Bessie said. "I assume you have recent interviews with all of them for us?"

Andrew nodded. "The key witnesses -- that is, the men and women who were with the victims at the party, as well as Joseph Sable – have all been interviewed multiple times since the night of the murders. According to Theodore, there's nothing in any of those interviews that is useful in any way."

"Maybe he's just too close to the case now, though," John said. "If he's talked to everyone year after year, maybe he's stopped really listening."

"That's a very good point," Harry said.

"I have those statements for you, and I also have a brief summary from Theodore as to what everyone is doing now," Andrew told them.

Bessie pulled out her notebook and pen. "Where are you going to start?" she asked.

"I'll start with Joseph. I'm going to tell you what each person is doing now, but I'm going to mostly skip over the things that happened to them over the past five years. There will be some exceptions, but, for most of the witnesses, you can read the details for yourselves later."

"So where is the bartender who poured the poisoned drinks?" Harry asked.

"He's living in Cornwall in a small fishing village," Andrew replied.

"Cornwall?" Doona echoed. "That's a big change from London."

"Was he that upset about the murders, or did he struggle to find work in London because of them?" Harry asked.

"Neither," Andrew replied. "The hotel kept him on after the murders, but he wasn't happy there any longer. After a year, he decided to take six months off to do some travelling. He was going to go from Land's End to John O'Groats."

"And he's in Cornwall?" Doona asked with a grin.

Andrew nodded. "He got down to Land's End and decided that he liked it there. Instead of travelling, he got a job running a tiny pub in a small village and when the six months were over, he decided to stay in Cornwall. He's worked at a couple of different pubs since, and he got married last year."

"Married? To someone he met in Cornwall?" Bessie asked.

"Married to the daughter of the man who owns the pub where he currently works," Andrew told her. "She's forty-seven and has been married twice before, but, according to Joseph, they're crazy about each other."

"How lovely for them," Bessie said.

"I hope he didn't do it," Doona said.

Bessie frowned. "He didn't have a motive for killing any of the victims."

"Maybe he was hoping to kill someone else, but that someone didn't get a glass of wine in time," Harry suggested.

"Let's move on," Andrew said. "Anyone want to guess where Naomi is now?"

"Probably involved with another man who is too old for her," Doona said.

Andrew chuckled. "Actually, it's the opposite. While she claims she didn't know that he'd done so, Dennis had recently changed his will, making Naomi his heir."

"Wow, that's weird," Doona said. "They'd only been seeing each other for a few months."

"And he had a short attention span," Harry said. "Did he change his will often?"

"According to his solicitor, Dennis changed his will every other month or so. His solicitor assumed that Dennis would be back soon to take Naomi out of the will, but, obviously, that never happened."

"So Naomi had a very strong motive after all," Harry said thoughtfully.

"Does that move her up your list of suspects?" Andrew asked.

Harry frowned. "Let's hear where everyone is now, and then I'll answer that."

"Naomi is living in Portugal. She bought a house there with the money that Dennis left her. Her boyfriend, who lives with her, is twenty-two," Andrew continued.

"Good for her," Doona said.

John grinned. "You could probably find yourself a younger man," he told her.

"I'm quite happy with the one I have," Doona replied softly.

John leaned over and kissed her cheek and then whispered something in her ear. Doona blushed and then giggled as John straightened back up.

"What about June? Where is she now?" Harry asked.

"She admitted in her initial interview that she knew that Laurence had already written a will with her as his main beneficiary," Andrew said. "Unfortunately for June, if that was true, no one has been able to find that will."

"Surely it shouldn't be hard to find," Bessie said. "What did his solicitor say?"

"He didn't have a solicitor that he used regularly," Andrew replied. "Theodore was able to find the man who'd drawn up a will for Laurence a year prior to his death. No one has been able to find a newer one than that."

"So where did his money go?" Harry asked.

"He left everything to a small local charity. June was upset, but we aren't talking about a great deal of money. He had a small life insurance policy through his work, and the contents of his flat," Andrew said.

"It probably would have been enough to make a difference for June," Bessie said, mindful of how little she'd inherited when Matthew, the man she'd loved, had died. She managed to make the money stretch for years, though, mostly thanks to smart investments by her advocate.

"She isn't still looking for another will, is she?" Charles asked.

Andrew shook his head. "She gave up after a year, maybe even less. According to Theodore, she's still quite bitter, but he reckons she's angry because Laurence lied to her, not because she believes the will is out there somewhere."

THE LAWRENCE FILE

"Interesting," Bessie said. "Is she bitter because she killed the man to get the money and then didn't actually get any?"

"That's one possibility, of course," Andrew said.

"So where is she now?" Harry asked.

"Still in the same place she was five years ago. In her most recent interview, she told Theodore that she'd recently met a new man but that it wasn't anything serious yet."

"What about Myra? She inherited whatever her sister had to leave, didn't she?" Doona asked.

"Actually, she didn't," Andrew said. "Brenda left everything to her former husband's only child. They'd been divorced for eleven years, and the child was only eight when Brenda died."

"What an odd choice," Hugh said.

"There is a copy of the will in the paperwork you'll be getting today, but, basically, Brenda said that she wanted her money to go to the next generation and that she knew that her ex-husband was a good person who would be raising a good child."

"They'd parted on friendly terms, then," Doona said.

"According to the ex-husband, they'd simply drifted apart. They'd also fought over children. Brenda didn't want them, but he did. He claimed to be blindsided by the bequest, but he was happy for his son. Again, it wasn't a great deal of money, but it will be a nice little nest egg for the child."

"I wonder if Myra was upset that she didn't inherit," Doona said.

"She told Theodore that she had no expectation of inheriting anything from her sister," Andrew said. "She'd received a large settlement in her divorce, anyway."

"And where is she now?" Bessie asked.

"Back with her ex-husband," Andrew told them.

Bessie's jaw dropped. "But she said such horrible things about him in her first interview. He kept her from seeing her sister and never let her have any fun. She said he was rude and demeaning and controlling."

"But he was there for her when her sister died under horrible circumstances," Andrew explained. "He arrived in London the next day and helped Myra make all of the necessary arrangements for Brenda. According to Myra, he was a rock, and the experience made her see him in a new light."

"So they got back together," Doona said.

"They did. They got remarried about six months after Brenda's death and they're still together today," Andrew said.

"That just leaves Olga and Lucy, the two at the top of our list of suspects," John said.

"Are they both still working for the same company?" Doona asked.

"Olga is, but Lucy left about four years ago. She got married just a few months after Brenda's death and quit working when she had her first child," Andrew said.

"Her first? How many does she have now?" Hugh asked.

"Three, with another on the way," Andrew replied.

"In four years?" Bessie asked.

"She had her first and then, eighteen months later, she had twins," Andrew explained.

"I thought the women were in their forties," Bessie said.

Andrew checked his notes. "Lucy is the youngest. She was thirty-eight when Brenda died."

"Now I'd hate to think that she's the killer," Doona said. "If she goes to prison, who will look after her children?"

"What do you know about her husband?" Bessie asked Andrew.

"Not a lot. I haven't read all of the interviews myself yet. I just have Theodore's summary. He noted that Lucy's husband is a few years younger than Lucy and that he'd been trying to get Lucy to go out with him for months before she finally said yes."

"So she got home from London, having seen a close friend get murdered, and decided to be less fussy about the men in her life," Doona suggested.

"Maybe," Andrew said. "See what you think when you read the interviews."

"What about Olga, then?" Bessie asked. "She's still at the same company?"

"She is. She got promoted about a year after Brenda's death and again more recently. She's now handling some of the biggest clients that the company works with and, thanks to a generous bonus scheme, is probably making more than twice what she was making five years ago," Andrew said.

"And would Brenda have been the one getting those promotions if she were still here?" Bessie asked.

"Theodore doesn't say. I don't know if he asked, but I'll make a note for him to do so," Andrew said.

"He should talk to Olga's supervisor, not just ask Olga," Harry said. "If Olga and Brenda were in competition for those jobs, though, then Olga had a pretty strong motive."

"You're assuming she would have known that they were competing against one another," Doona said.

"Olga struck me as a smart woman," Harry said. "I suspect she knew exactly where they all stood at work."

"Olga does seem very clever," Bessie said. "So much so that I'm not sure I can see her using such an imprecise method of killing someone."

"That is the problem, isn't it?" Harry asked. "But I still believe that one of the three people who died was the intended victim."

"Unless they were victims of a random madman," Doona said, "or madwoman, of course."

"So where does everyone go on your lists now?" Andrew asked.

"I'm eager to read the statements," Harry said. "I assume Theodore gave us the highlights, though."

"He seemed to think so, anyway," Andrew replied.

"But he may have missed something," John said. "We're hoping he's missed something."

Andrew nodded.

"My list is mostly unchanged," Bessie said after a moment. "I'm not certain what I want to do with Naomi, though."

"I'm leaving her at the bottom of my list until I've read all of her interviews," Doona said. "In the hours immediately following Dennis's death, she certainly didn't sound as if she thought she was his heir."

"Maybe she's just a good actress," Charles said.

"Maybe, but I'm reserving judgement until I've read what she's said in the years since," Doona said firmly.

"I've moved her up to the top of my list," Harry said. "I still think Olga needs a closer look, though, and I'd put Lucy right under her."

"I think I'd put Olga and Naomi together on one line, with Lucy under that," John said.

"I think Theodore should talk to Myra and Lucy again," Hugh said. "And I think he should ask them if they saw Olga do anything unusual while she was standing in the queue near the food."

"They've both been asked before if they saw anything," Andrew said.

"Yeah, but I think they should be asked specifically about Olga," Hugh said.

"So you still have Olga on the top of your list," Andrew said.

Hugh nodded. "She's been promoted twice since Brenda died. Maybe someone should ask Lucy what she thinks of that, too."

THE LAWRENCE FILE

Andrew made a note. "Charles, where is everyone on your list?"

"I'd like Theodore to show Naomi's picture to the other main suspects," he said. "I want to know if they remember seeing her at the party."

"So she's at the top of your list?" Andrew asked.

"She's definitely moved up from the bottom," Charles replied. "I'm not sure I'd put her at the top, though."

"Let's go over the questions we're sending to Theodore," Andrew said. "We want everyone questioned again, of course. The last set of updates that we have are from six months ago. Theodore usually reviews the case annually, so people might be surprised to see him again so soon."

"That might work in our favour," Harry said.

Andrew nodded. "I thought the same. He's going to start reinterviewing people tomorrow, starting with the main suspects. We should have the first reports from those conversations by Monday, when we'll meet again."

"I think he should focus on Naomi and Olga," Harry said.

"I think he should see if he can get Myra or Lucy to admit that she saw something that night," Hugh said.

"He can try to find out just how interested in Laurence's money June actually was," Charles said. "We don't have any statements from the family members or friends of the victims, aside from the ones who were at the party with them."

"There are some included in the paperwork you'll be getting today," Andrew said. "Theodore didn't conduct those interviews himself, but he did have officers in each area where the victims lived talk to their friends and family members."

"What about neighbours?" Harry asked.

"I'm not certain about that," Andrew said. "As I said, I haven't read the file yet, just the summary."

"What do you think the neighbours could tell you?" Hugh asked.

Harry shrugged. "Maybe someone who lived in the same building as Laurence and June knows something about the couple."

"Maybe Theodore should wait to talk to the suspects again until after we've read the updated statements," Bessie said.

Andrew shook his head. "Theodore wants to reinterview every single person involved in the case. He's coordinating efforts with constabularies across the country because very few of the witnesses are in London, but he's travelling a great deal this weekend to speak to the main suspects himself, and he's not going to want to try to rebook his travel plans now."

"But we're going to have more questions after we read the updates," Bessie said.

"And he's prepared to interview everyone a second time if he needs to," Andrew told her.

"He's trying to put pressure on the killer," Harry said. "I suspect he's going to tell all of the witnesses that a special team is now investigating the case."

Andrew nodded. "I don't expect the killer to suddenly get scared and confess, but maybe the extra pressure will cause him or her to make a mistake and say the wrong thing."

"Which would be the right thing for us," Doona said.

"Exactly," Andrew agreed.

"So he's going to go and interview everyone, telling them that the case is being reviewed by a special team of investigators," Harry said. "If he follows that up with another round of interviews just a few days later, it could be effective."

"I've already given him the list of the employees that you felt needed another look," Andrew said. "One of them passed away two years ago, but he's going to interview the other two himself."

"What about the people that we identified from the other party guests?" Doona asked.

"I do have updates on them, actually," Andrew said, looking through his notes.

"I bet Bill and Dorothy got divorced years ago," Doona said.

Andrew grinned at her. "You'd lose that bet," he said. "They are still together and, according to the inspector who interviewed them most recently, they're very happy."

"That surprises me," John admitted.

"You can read their statements yourself, but apparently the murders made them both realise how much they loved and appreciated one another. They both talk about suddenly understanding how close we all are to death and how random life can be," Andrew said.

"Interesting," Doona said.

"And what about Albert and Harold?" Bessie asked.

"They did get divorced," Andrew said with a chuckle. "By which I mean that they ended their business relationship. According to Theodore, they're still fighting their way through the courts, though, arguing over how to divide their various assets."

"What a shame," Bessie said.

"Is that all for today?" Harry asked.

Andrew looked around the table and then shrugged. "I don't have anything else to add. We don't have a lot of specific questions for Theodore, but we have some guidance for him. Hopefully, the interviews this weekend will give us more with which to work."

"I'm sure the statements you're giving us today will raise more questions," Bessie said as Andrew passed out two envelopes to each of them.

"No doubt," he agreed. "The thinner envelope contains the statements from the primary witnesses," he explained.

"The considerably fatter one contains all of the other statements. Most witnesses have only been questioned twice since the night of the murders, once a year after the party and then again about two years ago. Those two statements have been copied onto a single page for each witness."

"So only a hundred and fifty pages to read," Doona said.

Andrew nodded. "I glanced through them earlier, and most of the statements are short and unhelpful."

"Most of them were just innocent bystanders," Harry said. "I just hope we haven't missed anyone significant in the crowd." He took his envelopes from Andrew and headed for the door. "I'll see you all on Monday," he said as he reached it.

Charles wasn't far behind. The others chatted together as they packed up their bags.

"We are going to solve this one," Hugh said. "I just know it."

"I hope you're right," Andrew said as they all walked out of the conference room together.

CHAPTER 14

"Do you want to go anywhere before we head back to Laxey?" Andrew asked as he and Bessie got into his car.

She thought for a moment and then shook her head. "I'm eager to start reading all of the updates."

He grinned. "So am I, actually."

"We've all talked about where we'd put the suspects on our lists. Has Theodore ever shared his list with you?" Bessie asked as Andrew pulled out of the car park.

"He has, but I didn't want to mention it."

"Oh? What does that mean?"

Andrew chuckled "It means that his list is very different to ours."

"That's interesting. I'd love to hear his list, but if you don't want to tell me, that's fine."

"I don't mind telling you, as long as you promise it won't influence your thinking as you read the updated statements."

Bessie frowned. "I'd prefer to think that I would never let anyone else's opinion influence mine, but Theodore has actually met all of the people we're discussing. If he has others at the top of his list, he may well have good reasons for putting them there."

"Or maybe he simply took a dislike to someone and hasn't been able to see past that. Maybe that's the reason why the case remains unsolved."

Bessie thought for a minute and then sighed. "I want to know who is at the top of his list. I'll do my best not to let it influence me."

"He has Naomi at the top of his list."

"Naomi? Interesting."

"He has June second, and then the three women who were with Brenda all together in third place."

"Did he explain his reasons to you?"

"I believe he took a dislike to Naomi on the night of the murders."

"Because she was so clearly only involved with Dennis for his money?"

Andrew shrugged. "Maybe. And then she ended up inheriting his fortune. Theodore is convinced that she knew what was in Dennis's will before he died."

"Was she at the top of his list before Dennis's will was read?"

"From what I can determine, she's always been his number-one suspect. I believe June moved up the list because of her reaction to finding out that she wasn't actually Laurence's heir."

"And he's put the other three together? That seems odd, but maybe just because we're all rather focused on Olga."

"Theodore reckons that those three had the least likelihood of success. He told me that if he had to rank them, he'd put Myra at the top of that list, because she was the one who got the drinks. If it was one of the other two, she left an awful lot to chance."

Bessie sat back in her seat and closed her eyes. "They're at a party. They've all already had a drink or two. They get some food and carry it to a table near the centre of the room. I wonder if one of them hung back, maybe tried to find them a spot nearer to the bar at the back of the room."

"I can have Theodore try to take all three of them through the night again, minute by minute. They were all quite vague on the details in their initial statements."

"They were all upset on the night of the murders. I expect Theodore had them walk through the evening again in his follow-up interviews."

"I hope so, but it would have been best done as soon as possible after the murders."

"Maybe one of them would agree to be hypnotised," Bessie said thoughtfully. "I don't know if it actually works, but it might be something to try."

"It's an interesting idea. As you say, it would be interesting to know if one of them was a bit slower or maybe suggested staying closer to the food."

"And once they'd reached the table, I'd like to know exactly what was said," Bessie continued. "They all said that one of them mentioned needing drinks and that Myra offered to go to the bar. That suggests that it wasn't Myra who made the initial remark."

"Theodore really should have tried to pin down that entire conversation."

"He had hundreds of people to interview, and it doesn't sound as if he thought the conversation was all that important."

"No, he probably didn't. He was already more suspicious of other suspects."

"All three women said that Myra was the one who decided where to go to get the drinks," Bessie said, "I can't help but wonder if someone put the idea in her head."

Andrew sighed. "It's so incredibly risky. If Myra had

decided to go to a different bar, we'd have one fewer victim. Really, it only makes sense if Myra was the one who poisoned the bottle."

"Which seems to be the most logical conclusion. She got the first glass with the poison in it, after all. It would make sense that she added the poison to the bottle while she was waiting to be served. Then she got the drinks she needed and carried them back to the table. She probably didn't even realise that two people behind her both ordered glasses of the same wine."

"Naomi and Dennis were behind them in the food queue. Naomi could have poisoned the wine, knowing that Dennis was going to want a drink with his dinner."

"And June and Laurence were right behind them," Bessie said. "The same applies. I feel as if I'm talking myself out of suspecting Olga and Lucy, though. We should have talked this all through at the meeting."

"We walked through it during the reconstruction. We know every single suspect had the chance to poison the wine."

"But surely our killer wanted to be certain to kill the right person." Bessie shook her head. "I need to read the updated statements. Maybe I'll find something in those that helps."

"Read them with an open mind," Andrew told her. "Yes, if it was Olga or Lucy, she left a lot to chance, but maybe she was prepared to do that."

"Have Theodore ask Myra if Brenda ever said anything about other attempts on her life," Bessie said as the idea occurred to her. "Maybe this wasn't the killer's first try."

Andrew frowned. "Surely Myra would have said something to Theodore if that were the case."

"Maybe Myra didn't take it seriously. Maybe I'm grasping at straws. I just think he should ask, not just Myra, but Olga and Lucy, too."

"I'll add it to the list," Andrew said as he pulled up next to Bessie's cottage. "I assume you'd prefer to be left alone with your statements."

"I think I would, yes."

"Dinner at six?"

Bessie glanced at her watch and frowned. "It's already close to that now. How about dinner at seven?"

"We'll go somewhere nearby, so we aren't gone for long."

"Perfect," Bessie said as she got out of the car, holding onto her envelope tightly.

Andrew walked her to her door. She let herself in and then almost shut the door in his face in her eagerness to get to work. The light on the answering machine was blinking furiously.

She deleted a message from a local charity that she'd long ago decided not to support. The second message was more important.

"Bessie, it's Marion. Silvester didn't turn up for work today. Please ring me back. I'm not certain what to do now. Eugene wants to ring the police."

Dropping her envelope on the counter, Bessie picked up the phone. First she rang Andrew to let him know that Silvester was still missing. Then she rang Marion.

"Oh, Bessie, I just don't know what to do," Marion said after she'd picked up on the very first ring. "I kept telling myself not to worry, but Silvester never misses work. Eugene is very concerned, too."

"You know I had my friend Andrew see what he could discover. He's going to ring his associate in Liverpool and have him go and talk to Eugene."

"I assume this associate is with the police."

"He is, yes. He'll be able to take a proper missing person report from Eugene and then start searching for Silvester properly."

"I should have reported him missing on Sunday," Marion said sadly.

"The vast majority of missing adults turn up safely," Bessie told her. "It's still possible that he's with his new girlfriend and simply doesn't want to be found."

"Yes, I suppose that's possible."

"I'll ring you back if I hear anything from Andrew. As I said, his friend is going to talk to Eugene."

"That makes sense. Eugene knows more about Silvester's life in Liverpool than I do."

"Try not to worry too much."

"I'm afraid I can't help that."

Bessie sighed as she put the phone down. She couldn't help but worry either.

"I don't have time to worry about Silvester. I have a job to do," she said firmly before sitting down at the table with the envelope full of updated statements.

∽

When someone knocked on the door, Bessie jumped.

"Ah, is it time for dinner?" she asked as she opened the door to Andrew. "I've lost all track of time." A glance at the wall clock confirmed that it was seven.

"Helen has a late meeting, so she can't join us. While we eat, I'll update you on the search for Silvester," Andrew told her.

Bessie quickly got ready to go out and then followed Andrew to his car.

"Where shall we go?" he asked as he started the engine.

"How about the pub? It's close and it's usually reasonably quick."

Ten minutes later, they were sitting in a quiet nook in the

back of the dark pub. Bessie gave up on trying to read the menu by the light of the tiny candle on the table.

"I'll have shepherd's pie. That has to be on the menu."

Andrew laughed. "I think I'll just get the same."

When he came back from ordering at the bar, he brought drinks with him.

"What's happening in Liverpool, then?" Bessie asked after a sip of her fizzy drink.

"Wayne, my colleague there, has been to see Eugene. Silvester is now officially missing. Wayne sent a constable to Silvester's flat, but no one was there. He's got someone watching the flat where he believes Kalynn is staying. He's hoping to catch her going out so that she can be followed."

Bessie sighed. "Marion is terribly worried."

"He may still just be having a holiday."

"I know, but I'm worried, too."

Andrew's phone buzzed as their food was delivered.

As Bessie took a bite of shepherd's pie, Andrew checked the device.

"Kalynn just arrived back at the flat," he said. "Wayne hadn't gone home for the day, so he's heading over there now. He's hoping she'll be going out again soon, but if she stays the night, he's going to try to question her in the morning."

"I hope that isn't too late," Bessie murmured.

"We've no reason to suspect that Silvester has been the victim of foul play."

Bessie nodded, but she couldn't shake the feeling that something terrible had happened to her friend's brother.

"Have you found anything interesting in the updated statements yet?" Andrew asked after a minute.

"Not really. Theodore had Olga, Lucy, and Myra go back through the evening each time he spoke to them, but none of them offered anything specific. He also asked them all if any of them knew of any reason why anyone would want to harm Brenda, but he never actually asked them if there had ever been a previous attempt on her life."

"I sent him a long email with all of our questions, including that one. I suggested he might want to ask Naomi and June the same thing with respect to Dennis and Laurence, too."

"Yes, of course," Bessie agreed.

As they ate, the pair talked about snow and how much a part of Bessie's American childhood it had been.

"I think I'd rather skip pudding tonight," Bessie said as she finished the last of her drink. "I'm eager to get back to the statements, and I want to be home if Marion needs me."

Andrew nodded. "Let's go, then."

Bessie was silent on the drive back to Treoghe Bwaane. The cold case was a puzzle, but she felt fairly removed from it. Her worries about Silvester were much more pressing.

Andrew's phone buzzed again as he parked outside Bessie's cottage.

"Kalynn is on the move. Wayne is following her," he reported after he'd checked the device.

"I suppose that's good news. Do you want to come in for a cuppa?"

"I know you want to get back to work, but I might have updates for you throughout the evening."

"Why don't you get your copy of the file and then come over?" Bessie suggested. "We can work while we wait to hear from Wayne."

Andrew walked her to her door and then quickly walked through the cottage to make sure that everything was as it should be before he headed back to his own cottage to get his file.

Bessie used to hate it when her friends fussed over her in that way, but after her cottage had been broken into during a murder investigation, she'd come to appreciate their concern. While she waited for Andrew to return, she put the kettle on and filled a plate with biscuits.

"You said you had biscuits. You didn't say they were posh ones," Andrew said with a laugh as he took a seat at the kitchen table.

Bessie grinned. "I thought we needed chocolate-covered biscuits tonight."

"You aren't wrong."

Bessie was on her second cup of tea and her third biscuit when Andrew's phone buzzed again. She looked up from one of June's statements and watched as he checked the phone's screen.

"Wayne has followed Kalynn to another address. Let's just say he's familiar with the man who owns this particular property, and he's concerned as to why Kaylnn is there."

Bessie frowned. "I'm not sure I understand."

"Kalynn is visiting a known criminal," Andrew explained. "Wayne has called for backup. He's going to see if he can get inside the property."

"He's going to break in?"

Andrew chuckled. "He's going to knock on the door and ask to speak to Kalynn."

"I suppose that makes more sense."

"But it's less exciting," Andrew teased.

Bessie went back to June's statements, but she couldn't really concentrate. "What's taking so long?" she demanded a short while later.

Andrew looked up from his own pile of statements. "His backup probably hasn't even arrived yet."

Sighing, Bessie pushed the paperwork away and stood up. "I need a break. I can't think about anything except Silvester."

"Let's take a walk on the beach. That always clears your head, doesn't it?"

"It does, but I don't usually walk after dark."

"We don't have to go far."

"Just as far as the rock," Bessie suggested.

There was a large rock right behind Bessie's cottage. It was the perfect size and shape for two people to sit on, weather permitting.

The night was cool, and Bessie was glad she'd pulled on an extra layer. She and Andrew walked down to the rock and sat facing the sea.

"The tide is mostly out," Bessie said. "We'll need to watch it, though, so we don't get wet feet when we head back."

"The moon is very bright tonight."

"Or it feels bright because it's the only light we have."

"Maybe. It's nearly full. That helps."

Bessie looked at the row of cottages behind them. "It looks as if there are only a few occupied cottages."

"There will be even fewer next month."

"I do hope you'll find an easier case for us for next month."

Andrew sighed. "This one has been just as bad as I'd feared it would be. I'm sorry now that I picked it."

"You must have thought that we had a chance of solving it."

"I did, but some of it was just sheer nosiness," Andrew admitted. "I've stayed in that hotel, and I was incredibly eager to read the case file."

"And you can't just read case files whenever you want?"

"No, I can't, not any more than you or any other member of the public can. I get summaries from people who are interested in working with the unit, but I don't get the entire file until I agree that we'll consider the case."

"I didn't realise that."

He shrugged. "I don't have to tell you how sorry I am that I agreed to consider this one."

"We might still find something. I have a lot more statements to read."

"And we might get a lucky break, too. Maybe guilt has been eating away at someone for the past five years. Maybe when Theodore goes back to interview him or her again, that someone will confess."

"We keep saying him or her, but all of the main suspects are women."

"Aside from the bartender."

"Yes, but I don't think any of us consider him a serious suspect."

"Theodore doesn't either, but he's still on the list."

Bessie nodded. "We never talked about where the poison came from. You said it isn't hard to get."

"Theodore concluded that anyone at the party could have obtained it from a variety of sources."

"And the police never found the bottle or whatever container was used to bring the poison to the party?"

"They did not. They estimated that the killer only added about forty milliliters of poison to the bottle. That was more than enough to make the wine deadly, but it could have been contained in a very small bottle."

"Which the killer could have kept in a pocket for the rest of the evening and then discarded anywhere."

"The police did ask everyone to empty their pockets and handbags, but it was voluntary."

Bessie nodded. "I remember reading that. No one refused, but that doesn't prove anything. The killer could have done just about anything with the bottle before he or she was questioned."

"Indeed."

"As ever, I wish I could go across and talk to everyone myself."

"I know. That's the most difficult part of being in the unit."

"It's probably more difficult for you, since you used to actually be the inspector asking the questions. I've always just been nosy."

Andrew chuckled. "I, for one, am very grateful that you've always taken a keen interest in other people's lives. You're smart and you understand people, and it's made you an incredibly valuable part of the cold case unit."

Bessie flushed. "I'm glad I'm able to help. As frustrating as the unit can be, I'm pleased to have played a part in putting several killers behind bars."

Before Andrew could reply, his phone buzzed. He glanced at the screen and then frowned.

"I need to ring Wayne," he said.

Bessie frowned as Andrew got off the rock and pressed a few buttons on his phone.

"It's Andrew Cheatham," he said in his senior policeman's voice as he walked away.

"This can't be good," Bessie muttered as she watched the man walk up the beach. After a few minutes, she slowly climbed off the rock. The tide was coming closer, or at least that was the excuse she was going to use if she needed one. She stretched and then began to walk back towards her cottage. She hadn't gone far before Andrew suddenly turned around and walked back towards her.

"They've found Silvester," Andrew said. "He's on his way to hospital now."

CHAPTER 15

"Hospital?" Bessie gasped. "What happened to him?"

"Let's talk inside," Andrew suggested. "It's quite cold out here now."

Back inside Treoghe Bwaane, Bessie refilled the kettle and switched it on. Andrew was still using his phone, sending text messages back and forth as she prepared the tea.

"Should I ring Marion?" Bessie asked as she put the teacups on the table.

"Wayne has already spoken to her. She'd already bought herself a ticket for tomorrow's first ferry to Liverpool. She told him that she didn't know what she was going to do when she got there, but she was determined to do something."

Bessie grinned. "That's very much something Marion would do."

"Well, now she knows exactly what to do when she gets there."

"You said Silvester is in hospital?"

"He is, and he has a police guard as well."

"Where did they find him, and what's wrong with him, and is he going to be okay, and..." Bessie trailed off as Andrew held up a hand.

"Let me tell you what I know. That may or may not answer all of your questions."

Bessie nodded and then picked up her cup and took a slow sip of tea to stop herself from demanding answers more quickly.

"I told you that Wayne was waiting for backup before he was going to knock on the door and ask to speak to Kalynn," Andrew began.

Bessie nodded, keeping her lips pressed together to keep herself quiet.

"When his backup arrived, he did just that. When he asked for Kalynn, the butler invited him to come in and wait in the drawing room."

"The drawing room? You said this was a criminal's house."

"It is," Andrew said flatly.

"A very wealthy criminal, then."

"One who is very skilled at manipulating people and circumstances in such a way as to avoid ever having any charges brought against him. The local police know he's been behind any number of criminal acts, but they can't ever gather enough evidence against him to prove it in court."

"I'd always hoped that such people only existed in fiction."

"Unfortunately, they are very real. Fortunately for the police, many of them get increasingly complacent or even overconfident. Most of them end up in prison eventually."

"So what happened in the drawing room?" Bessie demanded.

"After a short while, Kalynn walked in. She told Wayne she couldn't imagine why the police wanted to speak to her, but that she would be more than happy to answer his questions."

"And then she told him where to find Silvester?"

"Not at all. Wayne started by asking her for her address. She said she was moving between the houses of various friends at the moment, including the one who owned the house where they were sitting. Then she asked him how he'd found her."

"What did he say?" Bessie asked as Andrew paused for a sip of his drink.

"He said that he'd been looking for someone else in the area and had just happened to see her. He then told her that he'd been looking for her in connection with a different case to the one that had brought him to the neighbourhood. While they were talking, Wayne sent a constable to knock on the back door."

Bessie grabbed a biscuit and took a bite to stop herself from demanding that Andrew talk faster.

"The butler opened the back door, which just happened to open into the kitchen. The constable was able to see Silvester sitting at the kitchen table. When the constable informed the butler that the man behind him had been reported missing, the butler slammed the door in the constable's face."

"My goodness!" Bessie exclaimed.

"There wasn't much he could do about Wayne, though. Wayne had been invited into the house, and the constable now notified him that he'd seen a missing person in the kitchen. Wayne told Kalynn and the butler that he wasn't leaving without Silvester and that if they did anything to interfere, he'd bring charges against them and the owner of the property."

"Did they just let Silvester leave, then?"

"That would have been too easy," Andrew said with a

grin. "They actually tried to sneak him out of the house. They took him through the basement and then up through an access tunnel that opened into the garden. Fortunately for Wayne, he knew about the tunnel and had a pair of constables waiting at the exit."

"I do hope everyone involved is going to prison," Bessie said.

Andrew shrugged. "A lot will depend on what Silvester has to say when he's able to speak."

"Able to speak? Is he okay?"

"He babbled incoherently at Wayne in the police car all the way to hospital. The doctors seem to think that he'd been given both alcohol and drugs."

"The Silvester I knew never touched drugs."

"His sister said the same thing."

Bessie frowned. "I don't understand. Why was Silvester in that house? Were they trying to get him hooked on drugs?"

"I don't think so, and neither does Wayne. We suspect that he was being kept there to cook for the household."

"To cook? They kidnapped him to make him cook for them?"

"We'll know more when Silvester starts feeling better, but that's definitely one possibility."

"If they wanted him to cook for them, why didn't they just offer him the job?"

"Because if they kept him there, a bit drunk and slightly off-kilter with drugs, they wouldn't have to pay him," Andrew suggested.

"But that's just horrible."

"And it may not be what was happening, but we won't know anything for certain until Wayne can talk to Silvester."

"I'll sleep better tonight knowing that he's somewhere safe, anyway."

Andrew nodded. "And now we can both turn our attention back to the cold case."

Bessie frowned. "Do we really have to?"

The pair sat and read through statements together until Bessie was struggling to keep her eyes open.

"I can't read another word," she told Andrew. "It's all getting muddled up in my head as it is."

"We both need sleep. The unit isn't meeting again until Monday. We have all weekend to read statements."

"I've read them all, though, and I don't think I've learned anything."

"So let's go to Peel Castle tomorrow. The change of scenery will do us both some good."

"Maybe Helen can come, too."

"It's Saturday. She shouldn't have to work."

∽

Bessie's internal alarm woke her just before six. A steady rain was falling outside her window. She frowned at it and then slowly got ready for her day. The rain hadn't stopped by the time she'd showered, dressed, and had some breakfast.

"Just a short walk, then," she muttered as she pulled on her waterproofs and her wellington boots.

As she stepped outside, she saw Andrew waving to her from the back of his cottage.

"Maybe not Peel Castle," he said, with a glance at the sky.

"What should we do today, then?" she asked.

"What about the House of Manannan? Then, if the weather clears, we can go to the castle in the afternoon," Andrew suggested.

"Yes, please," Helen called from across the room.

The trio spent the morning at the museum and then enjoyed lunch at the museum's café. As they emerged from the building, Bessie frowned at the clouds, which were still dropping rain.

"As much as I love Peel Castle, this is not the weather for attempting a visit," Bessie said.

"I think we should head back to Laxey," Andrew replied. "Maybe it's better there."

"I have cards," Helen said in the car on the drive. "If it's raining in Laxey, we can play cards all afternoon, and then I'll cook spaghetti for dinner."

It was still raining in Laxey. Bessie won a few hands of Crazy Eights, but Helen won the most. Then she made spaghetti, with salad and garlic bread. Andrew walked Bessie home.

"It's been a long and frustrating day," she said after he'd checked her cottage. "I don't suppose you can ring Wayne and ask for an update?"

"He texted me earlier to say that Silvester's doctors have told him to come tomorrow morning to get Silvester's statement. The drugs he was given need time to work their way through his system."

Bessie opened her mouth to reply, but she was interrupted by the telephone.

"Hello?"

"It's Marion."

"Hello. How are you? And how is Silvester?"

"I'm fine now. And Silvester is going to be fine. He's mostly embarrassed."

"Embarrassed?"

"Yeah, because he thought Kalynn was really interested in him, but she was really just looking for an easy target."

"Oh?"

"When they met, he didn't tell her about me. She said something about being alone in the world, and he replied that he was in the same position. He was just trying to make it seem as if they had something in common, but she assumed that that meant that no one would miss him if he disappeared."

"But what about Eugene?"

"They wanted him to ring Eugene and tell him he wasn't coming back. He was supposed to do it on Friday, but he told them he wouldn't do it. He said he could hear them talking after he'd said no. The butler told Kalynn that he'd just increase the dosage until Silvester became more agreeable."

"What were they giving him?"

"I've no idea, but Silvester knew he didn't want it. It took him a while to start being suspicious. He and Kalynn were supposed to go away for a few days. Kalynn made all of the arrangements, though, and then she insisted that they stop at a particular house on their way out of town."

"The house where Silvester was found?"

"Yup. Once they were there, Kalynn asked Silvester if he could make dinner for her friends to thank them for letting her stay with them. He didn't see any reason to refuse. He cooked dinner and then, while they were eating, the butler kept pouring him drinks."

"And he didn't think to say no."

"He woke up the next morning in a small room with no windows. The door was locked, but at least he had a tiny bathroom. He said he got sick and then vowed to never drink again. Of course, he says that a lot."

"Of course."

Marion sighed. "He said it again last night, and this time I think he really means it. They were keeping him there and making him cook breakfast and lunch and dinner every day. Whenever he complained, they gave him a shot of something that made him forget why he was complaining."

"Poor Silvester."

"Of course, he loves to cook, so once he'd forgotten to

complain, he'd just get on with it. He said there was some really posh guy who kept telling him what a good job he was doing. He said he told him that he didn't want to be there, that he was being kept there against his will, but the posh guy just laughed."

"That's interesting."

"Silvester is going to talk to the police tomorrow. Then he's coming back to the island with me for a few weeks. Obviously, I want him to move back so I can keep an eye on him, but he has to make his own decisions."

"At least you'll get his company for a few weeks."

"There is that. But I really rang to thank you. I can't tell you how grateful I am to you and your friend."

"We were happy to help."

Marion thanked Bessie at least a dozen more times before Bessie finally managed to end the conversation. Andrew was happy to hear everything that Marion had said.

"I'm glad we were able to help," he said when Bessie was finished. "What should we do tomorrow?"

Bessie sighed. "I should probably spend more time with the cold case file."

"That makes two of us," Andrew said, making a face.

When Bessie opened her eyes the next morning, it was half six. She gasped and then sat up in bed.

"Even my subconscious doesn't want to read those statements again," she muttered to herself as she got out of bed.

An hour later, after breakfast and a short walk in the pouring rain, she poured herself another cup of the coffee that had sounded so good over breakfast. Then she picked up her pile of statements and sat down at the table.

"Maybe I need to approach this differently," she said.

"Maybe I should try reading the first and the follow-up statements from the staff. I haven't read those yet."

She was still sorting through the various documents when her phone rang.

"It's Andrew. We're having an extra meeting in an hour at my cottage," he said.

"Something has happened."

"Indeed. The case is by no means solved, but we have some things to discuss."

"Do you need me to ring anyone?"

"I've already spoken to everyone else. Just be here in an hour."

A loud click followed his words. Bessie frowned as she put down the receiver. "What do I do now, then?" she asked loudly. When no one replied, she put the papers into neat piles and then put them into envelopes. She'd take them with her to the meeting, but, in the meantime, there seemed little point in going through them. Instead, she curled up with a book and tried to get lost in a fictional world.

When she shut the book forty minutes later, she was very aware that she hadn't actually read a single page. Her mind was racing as she went up the stairs to get ready to go out.

"Hello," Andrew said when she knocked on his door ten minutes later. "Come in and join the others. I'm just waiting for a text, and we'll get started."

Bessie grinned as she followed the man into the cottage's sitting room. "I thought I was too early," she said. "I didn't expect to find you all already here."

"I think we're all eager to hear what's happened," Doona said.

Andrew nodded. "I just need..." He trailed off as his phone buzzed. He read the screen and then shrugged. "Okay, well, that's not good news, but we can get started anyway."

Bessie sat down next to Hugh on the couch as Andrew walked over and sat in the only empty chair in the room.

"Where's Helen?" Charles asked.

"She went into Ramsey to do some grocery shopping," he explained. "She actually left before I called this meeting, so she could be back at any time."

"Talk fast," Harry suggested.

"You all know that I sent a list of questions to Theodore on Friday evening. One of those questions was one that Bessie suggested on our drive home from the last meeting. She suggested that I ask Myra if Brenda had ever complained about attempts on her life."

"Surely Myra would have mentioned them if she had," Doona said.

"Maybe not, if she was the one trying to kill her sister," Hugh said.

"But someone had made a previous attempt?" Harry asked Andrew.

"Not exactly," he replied. "When Theodore asked Myra that question, she shook her head and said no, but then she said, 'Someone tried to kill me, though, a month later.'"

"And she never bothered to mention it to the police?" Charles asked.

"According to Theodore, she just kind of laughed after she'd said it. When he asked her what she meant, she told him that about a month after her sister's death, she'd taken Brenda's car to a garage because she wanted to sell it. On the way there, the brakes failed. She crashed into a fence and had to have the car towed away. It was totally destroyed, so she simply collected the insurance money."

"What makes that an attempt on her life?" Hugh asked.

"She said that when the tow truck driver arrived, he looked at the car and suggested that maybe the brake lines had been cut. She said she didn't really think about it because she knew the car had been sitting in the airport car park for around six weeks. It was an older car, and she didn't think that Brenda had taken very good care of it, so she just assumed he was kidding. It wasn't until Theodore asked her that question that she started to wonder if someone had been trying to kill her."

Bessie stared at him. "Surely a more logical conclusion would be that someone had been trying to kill Brenda," she said.

Andrew nodded. "That was my thought, and Theodore's too. When he suggested that to Myra, he said she went pale and then started to cry."

"So someone was trying to kill Brenda," Harry said. "I wonder if the brake lines were cut at the airport or if they'd been cut before that and just hadn't managed to leak enough brake fluid to cause an accident yet."

"Is that possible?" Bessie asked.

"It depends on what's actually done to the lines," Andrew told her. "It's possible that the person who did it just punctured them, hoping that that would make the leak look accidental. If that person knew that the car was going to be sitting in one place for several days, he or she probably assumed that the fluid would drain slowly during that period."

"Of course, this all happened five years ago," Harry said. "The car will be long gone, along with any evidence."

Andrew nodded. "That text was from Theodore. He reached out to the tow company on Guernsey. Their records show that the car was towed to their facility and then taken apart for scrap."

"And the man who made the comment probably didn't remember it," Harry guessed.

"Worse, he passed away last year," Andrew said.

Bessie sighed. "Does this put us any closer to a solution, then?"

"It definitely gives Theodore something to work with when talking to Olga and Lucy. He spoke to them yesterday, but he's going to go back today and see them again. He should be doing that now, actually."

"He needs to ask them both if they remember anything about the airport car park on the day they all left for the party," Harry said.

Andrew nodded. "It's a line of questioning that hasn't been brought up before, anyway. He's quite excited to have something new to discuss with them."

"Neither of them will remember anything," Charles predicted.

"What now?" Harry asked.

"Now we wait. Theodore is going to talk to Lucy first and then Olga. He'll text me if he learns anything interesting. You are all welcome to go and get on with your lives. I can ring you if anything exciting happens."

"Or, we could just wait here with you," Charles said.

Andrew nodded. "We have cards."

Helen got home a short while later. If she was surprised to find the cottage full of people, she hid it well. Once she'd unpacked her shopping, she made tea and coffee and put out plates full of biscuits and cakes. The group sat around, talking about nothing much, while the tension in the room slowly rose. When Andrew's phone finally rang, everyone jumped. He checked the screen and then left the room.

"You're smiling," Bessie said when he walked back into the room a short while later.

"Olga confessed," Charles guessed.

Andrew shook his head. "It isn't going to be that easy, but we're getting closer to a solution."

"I suppose I should go to my room," Helen said. She got

her feet and walked to the door. "Congratulations on solving another case," she added before she left the room.

"Did Lucy remember something?" Charles asked as Andrew sat back down.

"She remembered a great deal," Andrew replied. "It was cold and rainy on the morning that they left for London. She drove herself to the airport and parked in the car park. As she got out of her car, she saw Olga parking a few rows away. She waved and then caught up to her so that they could walk together. She even remembered walking past Brenda's car and commenting to Olga that Brenda had beaten them to the airport."

"And then Olga dropped to the ground with a huge knife and rolled under Brenda's car," Hugh said as Andrew stopped to take a sip of tea.

"Almost," Andrew told him. "They hadn't gone much further when Olga remembered that she'd left one of her cases in her car. She told Lucy to go ahead and that she'd catch up. They had plenty of time, so Lucy didn't worry about it. She went and checked in for the flight and then went through security and found Brenda and Myra. They were having a drink at the bar when Olga finally found them."

"So Olga had plenty of opportunity to cut the brake lines," Hugh said.

"Also interesting is that Olga was wearing different clothes when she joined them," Andrew said. "Lucy asked her about it and Olga told them that she'd slipped in the mud, so she'd changed into one of the outfits from her suitcase. She said she always brought an extra outfit, so it didn't matter."

"And she's had five years to get rid of the clothes that she was wearing when she slid under Brenda's car and cut the brake lines," John said with a sigh.

Andrew nodded. "Theodore is on his way to question Olga now."

"If she was expecting Brenda to crash her car when she got back to Guernsey, why poison her in London?" Bessie asked.

"Maybe she was hedging her bets," Hugh said. "You know, just trying anything and everything to get rid of the woman."

"Maybe she wasn't trying to kill Brenda at the party," Doona said. "Maybe she wanted to kill a few people and upset everyone so that when Brenda crashed her car on the way home from the airport, everyone would say how sad Brenda had been."

"We could speculate all night," Andrew said. "I'm really hoping that Theodore will get Olga to explain it all."

When Andrew's phone buzzed an hour later, he frowned at the screen.

"Olga denies everything," he told them. "She said she didn't actually fall in the mud at the airport, that she changed because Lucy was wearing an outfit that was similar to hers and that she didn't want to be seen in public that way. She also claimed to be shocked and saddened to hear that someone might have cut Brenda's brake lines."

"That's a good story, actually," Doona admitted.

"She's had five years to get her story straight," John said.

"We'll meet tomorrow as scheduled," Andrew said. "We need to keep working through the case as if none of this is relevant, because it may not be."

Bessie sighed as she got up. "Back to the statements, then," she said sadly.

"Let's get dinner first," Andrew suggested. "Anyone else want to get dinner somewhere?"

In the end, they all went to the Seaview and had a delicious meal. Because Helen was there, they couldn't talk about the case, which suited Bessie. After a rich and delicious pudding, Andrew drove Bessie and Helen back to Laxey.

"Take the night off," he urged Bessie after he'd checked her cottage. "We can spend the morning going through statements together."

Bessie didn't need much persuading. After Andrew left, she tried again with the book she'd started earlier and found that she enjoyed it very much.

∽

As promised, Bessie and Andrew spent the morning going through statements. They ate lunch with Helen and then were halfway to Ramsey when Andrew's phone rang. He pulled over to the side of the road to answer.

"I'll ring you back in ten minutes," he told the caller before driving them to the Seaview.

While Bessie headed up to the conference room, Andrew made his call. Everyone else arrived and filled plates with biscuits before Andrew finally walked into the room.

Bessie felt her heart sink as she looked at his face. "Something dreadful has happened," she said.

Andrew nodded and then took his seat at the head of the table. "Theodore went back to talk to Olga again this morning. He found the door to her flat ajar. When he went inside, he found that she'd ended her own life last night."

Bessie sat back in her chair, feeling stunned.

Doona frowned. "Why? I hope she left a note."

"She did leave a note. In it, she confessed to killing Brenda and Dennis and Laurence. She claimed that she wasn't trying to kill anyone, that she was just trying to cause enough issues for Brenda that she'd start making mistakes at work. She just needed Brenda to screw up one account.

That's all it would have taken to guarantee that Olga would get the next promotion."

Bessie blew out the breath she hadn't realised she'd been holding. "So she poisoned a bottle of wine and cut the woman's brake lines?"

"She claims in her note that she didn't realise the poison would kill anyone. She just wanted to cause a few upset stomachs. She thought the mixture she'd made up was mostly harmless."

"Or so she claims," Harry said.

Andrew shrugged. "I can't see that it matters, not now. For what it's worth, she didn't leave things to chance, either. She dumped some of the poison into the bottle behind the bar, but then she added more to Brenda's glass when Myra brought the drinks. She claimed she never expected anyone to analyse anything, because she expected people to think they just had food poisoning. She also said she thought that the mixture she'd used would take at least an hour to do anything to anyone."

"And the brake lines?"

"She was hoping that a crash would make the supervisors at work doubt Brenda's stability. She never expected the crash to kill her."

"I'm not sure I believe any of that," Bessie said.

"I believe she killed three people," Harry said.

Bessie nodded. "Oh, yes, that I do believe."

"Why confess now?" Doona asked. "Did she really think the police were closing in on her?"

"Apparently she did. She said it was the questions about the brake lines that made her realise that she was about to get caught. She still had the bottle of poison from five years ago. She said it was about half empty, but that she was sure that would be enough to end things for her."

"And she was right," Hugh said sadly.

"Theodore rang for an ambulance, but there was nothing they could do."

"I never want to solve cases this way," Harry said.

Andrew nodded. "It wasn't the ending any of us were hoping for. I suppose we've no need to have a meeting now."

They all sat together for a while, just staring at one another.

"The sun is trying to come out," Andrew said eventually. "Does anyone want to go to Peel Castle?"

Bessie reckoned it was probably raining on the other side of the island, but she didn't say a word as everyone else agreed that a trip to Peel Castle was the best way to spend their afternoon now that the meeting had been cancelled. When they got there, they walked around together in the rain until the castle closed for the night.

∾

"I'VE HAD a note from Theodore, thanking us for our help," Andrew told Bessie a week later when he came to her cottage one morning.

"I almost wish we hadn't helped," she told him.

He nodded. "You might feel better when I tell you that when he searched Olga's flat, he found notes about heating and cooling systems and carbon monoxide. He also found evidence that she'd been following her immediate supervisor around lately, recording his every movement."

"She was planning another murder," Bessie said.

"It certainly looks that way."

"I'm almost afraid to ask what you have planned for us next month."

He grinned. "I expect next month's case to be a good deal easier."

"I hope you're right."

THE MOSS FILE

AN AUNT BESSIE COLD CASE MYSTERY

Release date: June 7, 2024

When Andrew comes back for another cold case meeting, he's cautiously optimistic about their chances of solving the case he's chosen. Douglas Moss was murdered and there are only four possible suspects. The problem is none of the suspects seem to have had a motive for killing Douglas.

As Bessie and her friends dig into the cold case, Bessie has something else on her mind. After living in her cottage for more years than she wants to admit, Bessie has just started to wonder how it got its name. Treoghe Bwaane means Widow's Cottage in Manx, but who was the widow?

The cold case unit has to sift through twelve years of follow up interviews, looking for missed hints as to what really happened in the Allegheny National Forest on the night that Douglas Moss died. Meanwhile, Bessie is spending her spare time in the Manx Museum archives, going through records that are considerably older. When she discovers that a man's body was found on Laxey Beach some twenty years before she bought her cottage, her suspicions immediately turn to murder.

A SNEAK PEEK AT THE MOSS FILE
AN AUNT BESSIE COLD CASE MYSTERY

Release date: June 7, 2024

Please excuse any typos or minor errors. I have not yet completed final edits on this title.

Chapter One

"Bessie, hello," Marjorie Stevens said as Bessie tapped on her open office door. "Come in and have a seat."

Bessie walked into the office and sat at one of the comfortable chairs in front of the woman's desk. As she got settled, she noticed the nameplate on the desk.

"Senior archivist? Is that a promotion?" she asked the pretty blonde woman.

Marjorie shrugged. "I think Manx National Heritage just decided that I needed a new title. There isn't any junior archivist and I'm still the librarian for the Manx Museum library, but they are paying me a few extra pence for my efforts."

"I'm glad to hear that. You work very hard."

"I suppose so, but I love what I do. When I was younger, I often imagined how wonderful it would be to spend all of my time surrounded by old documents, just immersing myself in history. Don't tell anyone, but if they stopped paying me, I'd still come to work every day."

Bessie laughed. "You definitely don't want anyone to hear you saying that."

"It's so good to see you. I was worried that we'd upset you in some way, when you stopped coming in to see us, but then I found out about the cold case unit, and it all made sense."

"The cold case unit does keep me very busy."

"The article in the local paper said that you spend a fortnight each month considering a cold case."

Bessie nodded. "Some members of the unit only come to the island for a week at a time. Once we've had some initial discussions about the case, they can go back to London and work from there if necessary." *But so far we've solved every case while they've still been on the island,* she added silently. She wasn't supposed to talk about how successful they'd been.

"I hope you have time for a long chat. I want to hear all about the cold case unit and how it works. The man who started it is a former Scotland Yard detective, isn't he?"

"Yes, Andrew Cheatham worked for Scotland Yard in the homicide unit. He retired a few years ago."

"How did you even meet him?"

"Ah, that's a bit of a long story. Do you remember me talking about going across to a holiday park with my friend Doona Moore some years ago?"

Marjorie nodded. "I believe you've gone more than once."

"Yes, we have now, but we met Andrew on our first visit. Doona was told she'd won a holiday at the park in a contest."

"I do remember you telling me that. She was very excited about winning and she invited you to join her at the park."

"Exactly, but when we got there, we discovered that she hadn't actually won the holiday. Her estranged husband had arranged for the holiday because he wanted to see her again."

Marjorie sighed. "Poor Doona."

"Sadly, the man was murdered before he and Doona had a chance to talk."

"This is all sounding vaguely familiar. There must have been some island gossip about all of this. Didn't Doona inherit a fortune from the man?"

"He did leave his entire estate to her. There were some life insurance policies, and he also left her small shares in various properties across the UK. The only thing that Doona kept was a share in the holiday park."

"Which explains why you keep going back."

Bessie nodded. "Doona goes back and forth quite a lot, actually. She spent a large part of the summer there, but she always comes back to the island for the cold case unit meetings."

"Of course, because she's part of the unit. I suppose that's why she quit working at the constabulary, then. When I heard she wasn't working there any longer, my first thought was that she's far too young to be retired."

Bessie grinned. "She's not quite fifty, so much too young to retire. I believe, if you ask her, that she'll tell you that managing the holiday park from here is a full-time job."

"And she was only a part-time receptionist at the constabulary. I did wonder if she found it awkward, working with Inspector John Rockwell after they'd become personally involved."

"I believe they both enjoyed working together, actually. Doona also helps John with the children, which takes up a lot of her time."

"Ah, those poor kids," Marjorie said. "Imagine your mother leaving your father for another man and then finding out that she never actually loved your father, that she was still in love with the other man, someone she'd been involved with years earlier."

"I'm not certain how much of the story they know," Bessie said, wondering why Marjorie knew so much of the story.

"It must have been a lot worse when their mother married the other man and then dumped them on the island with their father while she and her new husband went all the way to Africa for a very long honeymoon."

"I believe the children were happy to be left with John."

"Yes, of course, but then their mother passed away unexpectedly. That must have been dreadful for them."

Bessie nodded. "It was terribly sad. Thomas and Amy are doing great, though. John is a brilliant father and, as I said, Doona helps a great deal."

"As I understand it, Inspector Rockwell and Doona are very happy together."

"I believe so."

Marjorie shook her head. "But you were explaining how you met Inspector Cheatham."

"Was I?" Bessie laughed. "We have wandered off topic. It's quite simple, really. He was staying in the cottage next to where Doona and I were staying. When he discovered that we were involved in a police investigation, he offered to help."

"That was kind of him."

"He is very kind, but I think he was also quite bored at the holiday park and missing police work."

"I can understand that. I don't ever want to retire."

Bessie shrugged. "I've never held a paying job, so it's difficult for me to imagine giving one up."

"They are paying you to be on the cold case unit, though, aren't they?"

"We do get a stipend for the work that we do."

"But you received an inheritance when you were very young, didn't you? I remember you telling me about the man you loved and how he passed away on a sea journey to the island to come to see you."

Bessie swallowed the small lump in her throat that still appeared whenever she talked about Matthew Saunders. "Yes, Matthew and I met when I was living in the US. I was only seventeen and when my parents decided to return to the island, they insisted that I return with them. We'd left the island when I was only two years old, and I didn't remember it at all. I wanted to stay in America and marry Matthew, but they wouldn't hear of it."

"And when he died, he left you everything he had."

"It wasn't a lot, but it was enough to allow me to buy my cottage on the beach so that I no longer had to live with my parents. I blamed them for Matthew's death. My advocate invested what was left and by living very frugally, I never had to find work."

"And we've wandered off topic again," Marjorie laughed. "Tell me about Inspector Cheatham."

"As I said, he's been retired for years now. He has a large family with children, grandchildren, and great-grandchildren. His wife passed away years ago now. He has a flat in London, but he spends a fortnight each month on the island working with the cold case unit."

"Someone told me that he usually stays in one of the cottages on the beach near your cottage."

"He does. He likes being right on the water and from there it isn't a long drive to Ramsey. We typically have our meetings at the Seaview, which is where the other members of the unit who come in from London typically stay when they're here."

"I'm trying to remember what I read about the other

members," Marjorie said. "One of them is a homicide inspector, I believe."

"That's Harry Blake, but he's also retired."

"There were pictures in the paper. He looked rather unpleasant, really."

"He's not the least bit unpleasant, but he's also not terribly friendly, if that makes sense."

Marjorie nodded. "And the other inspector from London is an expert in missing persons, isn't he?"

"Charles Morris is one of the world's leading experts in finding missing people," Bessie said. "He's also retired, but he's in huge demand as a consultant. Harry does a lot of consultancy work, too, actually."

"I can see why they are both in the unit, then," Marjorie said. "And Inspector Rockwell is an excellent inspector who does a wonderful job policing Laxey and Lonan here on the island."

"He's very good at his job," Bessie agreed.

"And Doona used to work for the police, which is probably why she was asked to join the unit."

Bessie shook her head. "When Andrew was putting the unit together, he selected people that he knew could work well together to solve cases. John, Doona, Hugh, and I worked together to solve a lot of murders here on the island."

Marjorie shuddered. "There were quite a lot of murders in a very short space of time, weren't there? And you were involved in every case."

"Unfortunately."

"But you helped solve them all, which is the most important thing. And even better, there hasn't been a murder on the island in over a year."

"Thankfully."

"I'd forgotten that young Hugh Watterson was a part of the cold case unit. He's just a constable, isn't he?"

"He is, but he's taking classes at night, working towards a degree. He wants to be an inspector one day."

"Good for him, but when does he sleep? He and his wife have a small child, don't they?"

"They do, and Aalish is getting a little brother or sister in February."

"How exciting for them, but also how exhausting."

Bessie nodded. "Hugh manages to fit it all in. The constabulary gives him time off to be part of the cold case unit, which helps."

"The newspaper article hinted that the unit has had some success."

"We have had some success, but I can't really talk about anything that we do."

"I read in the London papers recently about a cold case there. After five years, the police had finally worked out who killed three people at a Christmas party at a London hotel."

"I read about that," Bessie said.

Marjorie raised an eyebrow. "Did you, now?"

"We look at cases from all over the world, and they aren't all murder investigations, either."

"And you aren't going to tell me if you solved the London hotel case or not, are you?"

"I suppose you're wondering why I'm here," Bessie said.

"And she changes the subject. I'm going to assume that your unit solved that case, then. Otherwise, you would have just denied any involvement."

"Someone asked me about the name of my cottage."

Marjorie laughed. "Okay, no more about the cold case unit, then. What about the name of your cottage?"

"It's 'Treoghe Bwaane,'" Bessie told her.

"Widow's Cottage in Manx. I can understand why you chose that name."

"But that's just it. I didn't choose the name. It was

already called Treoghe Bwaane when I bought it. My friend wondered why, which made me realise that I don't know."

Marjorie frowned. "I'm surprised that you never did any research into the history of your own cottage. You've spent so much time in our archives doing research into so many things."

"Perhaps oddly, I never really thought about it. I suppose when I first bought the cottage, I was so devastated to have lost Matthew that I wasn't thinking clearly. Over time, the name just became part of the cottage and I never thought to question it."

"And now you're questioning it."

"Now I'm curious. I'd love to find out more, but I'm not certain I can. I should have asked my neighbours on the beach about it when I first moved in, but I barely spoke to anyone in those days."

"I would imagine they're all gone now," Marjorie said thoughtfully.

Bessie nodded. "Thomas and Maggie Shimmin started buying cottages on the beach about twenty years ago with a plan to replace them with holiday cottages once they owned them all. It took them years to acquire every property on the beach, aside from mine, but once they'd managed it, they tore them all down and built the holiday cottages that are there now."

"And none of the former residents are still on the island?" Marjorie asked.

"Most of them passed away and their heirs sold the cottages to Thomas and Maggie. A few moved into care homes elsewhere on the island, but the last of my former neighbours passed away more than a year ago."

"How long have you lived in the cottage?"

Bessie frowned. She didn't like to think about her age. "More than sixty years," she said eventually.

"Do you still have the paperwork from the sale of the house? That would have the name of the previous owner on it."

"I don't believe I have any of that paperwork, but I'm certain my advocate must."

"That might be the best place to start. Of course we have Wood's Atlas. That would show you who owned the property in 1867 and tell you whether or not the cottage had that name back then."

Bessie nodded. "I should have thought of that myself."

"It's probably best to start with the most recent owners and work backwards. The Libri Vastarum is all on microfilm if you want to work your way through it."

"That's the book that records changes of ownership, isn't it?"

"It is, but it isn't completely indexed. You're probably better off starting with your advocate and working from there. Once you have a name, you can search the parish registers from more information about the owners."

"I'll talk to Breesha today."

"While you're getting that name, I'll have a look through Wood's Atlas and see what I can find. I'll also look through our archive catalogues and see if I can find any reference to Treoghe Bwaane."

"You have catalogues?"

"We're working on them. I have a team of students from the local college working in the archives with me. They've been going through everything and trying to catalogue more of our holdings. You know that we have boxes and boxes of documents and old papers from across the island. They're a wonderful resource, but they're useless as long as no one knows we have them.

Bessie knew exactly what Marjorie meant, because she'd spent some time cataloguing boxes of old papers for the museum herself. As a strictly amateur historian, Bessie had spent years studying wills and other old documents. Her job with the cold case unit had meant that it had been quite some time since she'd done any work with the museum, though.

"Please let me know if you find anything," Bessie said. "I'll see if I can get a name from Doncan."

"When you do, ring me and let me know what you've found. I can get one of my assistants to search the parish registers for Laxey for you."

"I don't want to give you more work to do. I can search the registers myself."

"When is your next cold case meeting?"

Bessie sighed. "Andrew and the others are flying across tomorrow morning. The unit will meet in the afternoon."

"And then you'll be busy for a fortnight."

"Maybe not a fortnight, but certainly for a week."

"It's up to you," Marjorie said. "Of course, you're welcome to do the research yourself, but I have assistants who can help while you're busy with the cold case unit."

"Let me see what I can get from Doncan. I can decide from there."

"And while you're doing that, I'll see if we have anything in the archives that might be of interest. I know we got a dozen or more boxes from an old house in Laxey that was about to be torn down. The attic was full of boxes of old papers which we were happy to take. I don't know that there will be anything useful to you in them, but you never know."

"I know which house you mean. It was a large property right on Laxey Harbour, so quite near to my cottage. I suppose it's possible that there was some connection between the family that owned the house and the owners of my cottage."

"Oh, I do hope so," Marjorie said. "I'm almost as eager as you are to find out who named your cottage and why."

Bessie chuckled. "I think it's a bit optimistic to think we'll be able to find out that much."

"How old was the cottage when you bought it?"

Marjorie grabbed a pen and a notebook and looked at Bessie expectantly.

"I'm not certain, but it had been there for some time, maybe fifty years, maybe a hundred."

"So there might have been several previous owners, and any one of them might have named the cottage."

Bessie nodded. "And we may not be able to learn much about any of them."

"I shall have a think about other resources in the archives that might help. Ring me when you have a name for the previous owner."

"I will, and thank you for your help."

Bessie stood up and then, after Marjorie got up, too, gave the woman a hug.

"And come and visit me more often," Marjorie said as she walked Bessie out of the office and down the corridor. "You know you're always welcome."

"I know, but I feel quite guilty coming here when I'm not here to work."

"You worked very hard for us for many years, and now you work very hard for Scotland Yard. I'm just proud to tell people that I know you."

Bessie shook her head at the thought. "I'll ring you soon," she promised as Marjorie opened the large wooden exit door.

"Please do."

There were a dozen stone steps from the doorway to the car park. When Bessie reached the ground, she turned and began a slow stroll back towards the centre of Douglas.

"And since I'm in the neighbourhood, I might as well go and visit Doncan rather than ringing him," she decided.

A short while later, she was sitting comfortably across a desk from Breesha, Doncan's assistant, with a cup of tea and small plate of biscuits in front of her.

"Before you arrived, I was just looking for an excuse to take a break and have a biscuit or two," Breesha told Bessie. "I'm ever so glad you're here."

Bessie laughed. "You don't even know what I want."

"That's very true, but once I've had a cuppa and a biscuit, I'll be ready for anything."

The pair chatted about the unseasonably cold weather they'd been having since late September.

"I do hope it improves before Hop-tu-Naa," Bessie said. "I hate to imagine the children going door-to-door when it's so cold."

Breesha nodded. "We've over a fortnight to go before Hop-tu-Naa, though. I'm sure the weather will improve by then. But what brings you in today? I do hope that nothing is wrong."

"Nothing is wrong. I've just been wondering about my cottage, that's all."

"Wondering about your cottage?"

"Wondering about its name. It's called 'Treoghe Bwaane,' which is Manx for 'Widow's Cottage.' I've been wondering why it was given that name."

Breesha frowned. "Do you think Doncan or his father might know?"

"I doubt it, but I was hoping you might still have the paperwork from when I bought the cottage. That would at least give me the name of the sellers."

"Ah, and then you can do some research and see what you can find."

"Exactly."

"When did you buy the cottage?" As soon as she asked the question, Breesha flushed.

A SNEAK PEEK AT THE MOSS FILE

Everyone who knew Bessie knew that she was sensitive about her age.

"Never mind that, it will all be in your file," Breesha said quickly. "The problem is, a lot of the older files aren't kept here any longer. They're all safe enough, but they're kept in a storage unit in Jurby. There isn't enough space here for all of the paperwork that multiple generations of advocates have generated."

"Advocates are rather fond of paperwork."

"You can say that again," Breesha said, glancing at the pile of papers beside her on the desk.

"Does that mean that you can't help me?"

"Oh, no. Of course, I'll help, but it may take a few days. I'll need to drive up to Jurby and then go through dozens of old filing cabinets until I find the right one. I'll talk to Doncan later today to when he can spare me this week or next. I'll ring you as soon as I have any information."

"I didn't mean to cause you so much bother."

"It's no bother at all. I'm quite pleased to have a chance to get away from my desk for a day, anyway. Digging through old files in Jurby sounds almost as if it will be a holiday."

They talked for a short while longer before Breesha's phone rang. As she reached for it, Bessie gathered up her things.

"Thank you," she said quickly.

"I'll ring you," Breesha promised before she picked up the receiver.

ALSO BY DIANA XARISSA

The Isle of Man Cozy Mysteries

Aunt Bessie Assumes
Aunt Bessie Believes
Aunt Bessie Considers
Aunt Bessie Decides
Aunt Bessie Enjoys
Aunt Bessie Finds
Aunt Bessie Goes
Aunt Bessie's Holiday
Aunt Bessie Invites
Aunt Bessie Joins
Aunt Bessie Knows
Aunt Bessie Likes
Aunt Bessie Meets
Aunt Bessie Needs
Aunt Bessie Observes
Aunt Bessie Provides
Aunt Bessie Questions
Aunt Bessie Remembers
Aunt Bessie Solves
Aunt Bessie Tries
Aunt Bessie Understands
Aunt Bessie Volunteers
Aunt Bessie Wonders

Aunt Bessie's X-Ray

Aunt Bessie Yearns

Aunt Bessie Zeroes In

The Aunt Bessie Cold Case Mysteries

The Adams File

The Bernhard File

The Carter File

The Durand File

The Evans File

The Flowers File

The Goodman File

The Howard File

The Irving File

The Jordan File

The Keller File

The Lawrence File

The Moss File

The Markham Sisters Cozy Mystery Novellas

The Appleton Case

The Bennett Case

The Chalmers Case

The Donaldson Case

The Ellsworth Case

The Fenton Case

The Green Case

The Hampton Case

The Irwin Case

The Jackson Case

The Kingston Case

The Lawley Case

The Moody Case

The Norman Case

The Osborne Case

The Patrone Case

The Quinton Case

The Rhodes Case

The Somerset Case

The Tanner Case

The Underwood Case

The Vernon Case

The Walters Case

The Xanders Case

The Young Case

The Zachery Case

The Janet Markham Bennett Cozy Thrillers

The Armstrong Assignment

The Blake Assignment

The Carlson Assignment

The Doyle Assignment

The Everest Assignment

The Farnsley Assignment

The George Assignment

The Hamilton Assignment

The Ingram Assignment
The Jacobs Assignment
The Knox Assignment
The Lock Assignment

The Isle of Man Ghostly Cozy Mysteries

Arrivals and Arrests
Boats and Bad Guys
Cars and Cold Cases
Dogs and Danger
Encounters and Enemies
Friends and Frauds
Guests and Guilt
Hop-tu-Naa and Homicide
Invitations and Investigations
Joy and Jealousy
Kittens and Killers
Letters and Lawsuits
Marsupials and Murder
Neighbors and Nightmares
Orchestras and Obsessions
Proposals and Poison
Questions and Quarrels
Roses and Revenge
Secrets and Suspects
Theaters and Threats
Umbrellas and Undertakers
Visitors and Victims

Weddings and Witnesses
Xylophones and X-Rays
Yachts and Yelps
Zephyrs and Zombies

The Margaret and Mona Ghostly Cozies

Murder at Atkins Farm

The Sunset Lodge Mysteries

The Body in the Annex
The Body in the Boathouse
The Body in the Cottage
The Body in the Dunk Tank
The Body in the Elevator
The Body in the Fountain

The Lady Elizabeth Cozies in Space

Alibis in Alpha Sector
Bodies in Beta Sector
Corpses in Chaos Sector
Danger in Delta Sector

The Midlife Crisis Mysteries

Anxious in Nevada
Bewildered in Florida
Confused in Pennsylvania
Dazed in Colorado

The Isle of Man Romances

Island Escape
Island Inheritance
Island Heritage
Island Christmas

The Later in Life Love Stories

Second Chances
Second Act
Second Thoughts
Second Degree
Second Best
Second Nature
Second Place
Second Dance

BOOKPLATES ARE NOW AVAILABLE

Would you like a signed bookplate for this book?

I now have bookplates (stickers) that I can personalize, sign, and send to you. It's the next best thing to getting a signed copy!

Send an email to diana@dianaxarissa.com with your mailing address (I promise not to use it for anything else, ever) and how you'd like your bookplate personalized and I'll sign one and send it to you.

There is no charge for a bookplate, but there is a limit of one per person.

ABOUT THE AUTHOR

Diana has been self-publishing since 2013, and she feels surprised and delighted to have found readers who enjoy the stories and characters that she imagines. Always an avid reader, she still loves nothing more than getting lost in fictional worlds, her own or others!

After being raised in Erie, Pennsylvania, and studying history at Allegheny College in Meadville, Pennsylvania, Diana pursued a career in college administration. She was living and working in Washington, DC, when she met her future husband, an Englishman who was visiting the city.

Following her marriage, Diana moved to Derbyshire. A short while later, she and her husband relocated to the Isle of Man. After ten years on the island, during which Diana earned a Master's degree in the island's history, they made the decision to relocate again, this time to the US.

Now living near Buffalo, New York, Diana and her husband live with their daughter, a student at the University at Buffalo. Their son is now living and working just outside of Boston, Massachusetts, giving Diana an excuse to travel now and again.

Diana also writes mystery/thrillers set in the not-too-distant future as Diana X. Dunn and Young Adult fiction as D.X. Dunn.

She is always happy to hear from readers. You can write to her at:

Diana Xarissa Dunn
PO Box 72
Clarence, NY 14031.

Find Diana at: DianaXarissa.com
E-mail: Diana@dianaxarissa.com

Made in the USA
Columbia, SC
18 May 2024